"Howdy, ma'am."

She jumped at his greeting and smacked her head on the door frame, causing him to wince. Running a hand through her short, mousy brown curls, she backed out of the car with care and turned. One corner of his mouth went up in a half smile as her bespectacled gaze moved from his boots up to his face.

But his smile froze before it reached the other side of his mouth when his gaze collided with hers. Behind huge owlish glasses were eyes as green as summer grass, surrounded by long dark lashes. Trey's mouth went dry. He didn't know how long he stood staring into the emerald depths of her wide eyes. A thud at his dust-covered boot brought him back to his senses, and he looked down to see an overstuffed nylon bag at his feet.

"Let me—" he said, bending down to retrieve the tote.

"I can—" she said at the same time, whacking her head into his.

The blow brought him back to normal. He breathed in a sigh of relief that he'd broken contact with her hypnotic gaze.

Dear Reader,

When you're stuffing the stockings this year remember that Silhouette Romance's December lineup is the perfect complement to candy canes and chocolate! Remind your loved ones—and yourself—of the power of love.

Open your heart to magic with the third installment of IN A FAIRY TALE WORLD..., the miniseries where matchmaking gets a little help from an enchanted princess. In *Her Frog Prince* (SR #1746) Shirley Jump provides a rollicking good read with the antics of two opposites who couldn't be more attracted!

Then meet a couple of heartbreaking cowboys from authors Linda Goodnight and Roxann Delaney. In *The Least Likely Groom* (SR #1747) Linda Goodnight brings us a risk-taking rodeo man who finds himself the recipient of lots of tender loving care—from one very special nurse! And Roxann Delaney pairs a beauty disguised as an ugly duckling with the man most likely to make her smolder, in *The Truth About Plain Jane* (SR #1748).

Last but not least, discover the explosive potential of close proximity as a big-city physician works side by side with a small-town beauty. Is it her wacky ideas that drive him crazy—or his sudden desire to make her his? Find out in *Love Chronicles* (SR #1749) by Lissa Manley.

Watch for more heartwarming titles in the coming year. You don't want to miss a single one!

Happy reading!

Mavis C. Allen
Associate Senior Editor

Please address questions and book requests to:
Silhouette Reader Service
U.S.: 3010 Walden Ave., P.O. Box 1325, Buffalo, NY 14269
Canadian: P.O. Box 609, Fort Erie, Ont. L2A 5X3

The Truth About Plain Jane

ROXANN DELANEY

SILHOUETTE  Romance

Published by Silhouette Books

America's Publisher of Contemporary Romance

To Kathie, who always has faith in me and uses her size
5 to prove it. Thank you, Rosebud. And to the rest of the
Ditzy Chix—Belinda, Bron, Carol, Denise, Kristi,
Lindsey, Lisa, Marge, Mary and Roxanne—bless you all.
You're the best.

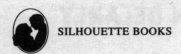 **SILHOUETTE BOOKS**

ISBN 0-373-19748-9

THE TRUTH ABOUT PLAIN JANE

Copyright © 2004 by Roxann Farmer

Books by Roxann Delaney

Silhouette Romance

Rachel's Rescuer #1509
A Saddle Made for Two #1533
A Whole New Man #1658
The Truth About Plain Jane #1748

ROXANN DELANEY

doesn't remember a time when she wasn't reading or writing, and she always loved that touch of romance in both. A native Kansan, she's lived on a farm, in a small town and has returned to live in the city where she was born. Her four daughters and grandchildren keep her busy when she isn't writing, designing Web sites or planning her high school class reunions. The 1999 Maggie Award winner is thrilled to have followed the yellow brick road to the land of Silhouette Romance and loves to hear from readers. Contact her at roxann@roxanndelaney.com, or at P.O. Box 16606, Wichita, KS 67216-1104. Also be sure to visit her Web site at www.roxanndelaney.com.

All underlined places are fictitious.

Chapter One

Sinking onto the leather chair behind the massive oak desk that proclaimed him head honcho, Trey Brannigan ran a hand down his face. The day wasn't over yet. Plenty of time for more to go wrong.

Now that he had all but one of the Triple B's guests deposited and settled in their respective cabins, all he wanted was some peace and quiet. But the view from the office window of the rust-eaten Mustang coming up the drive was a sure sign that it wouldn't happen until he'd settled the last of his guests.

Shoving himself from the chair, he headed outside to greet the latecomer. As he descended the wide steps of the ranch house porch and made his way to the parking area, he was subjected to the sight of a flower-covered backside at the open rear door of the ancient car.

Trey smiled to himself. It only stood to reason that

the latecomer was a woman. Women were good for a lot of things, but one thing was certain—they were inevitably late.

He chuckled to himself as he neared the tardy female. Her taste in clothes left a lot to be desired. Neon green, orange and yellow flowers danced invitingly before him as she wrestled with something in the back seat of her car. The sight would have been enticing if it hadn't been for the blinding colors.

"Howdy, ma'am."

She jumped at his greeting and smacked her head on the door frame, causing him to wince. Rubbing a head of short, mousy brown curls, she backed out of the car with care and turned. One corner of his mouth went up in a half-smile as her bespectacled gaze moved from his boots up to his face.

But his smile froze before it reached the other side of his mouth when his gaze collided with hers. Behind huge owlish glasses were eyes as green as summer grass, surrounded by long dark lashes. Trey's mouth went dry. He didn't know how long he stood staring into the emerald depths of her wide eyes. A thud at his dust-covered boot brought him back to his senses, and he looked down to see an overstuffed nylon bag at his feet.

"Let me—" he said, bending down to retrieve the tote.

"I can—" she said at the same time, whacking her head into his.

The blow brought him back to normal. He breathed in a sigh of relief that he'd broken contact with her hypnotic gaze. The scent of a summer garden drifted toward him. Intoxicating. Still bent over, he took a step back and was brought to a halt by the open car door. Grabbing the bag, he straightened, shaking his head to clear it from an unaccustomed buzzing sound, and glanced up at her.

She shoved the bridge of her glasses up with delicate fingers that trembled. "I—I'm so sorry."

"S'okay," he said, making sure he didn't look directly into her eyes. Sidestepping around her, he reached inside the car for two suitcases that were propped on the seat. "You must be M. Chastain," he said over his shoulder as he pulled the luggage out of the car and set it at his feet.

"My, uh, trunk lock is broken." Her tone was apologetic, and she quickly moved out of his way when he swung around to face her.

He simply nodded, avoiding a direct hit from her eyes, and then gestured with another nod in the direction of the cabins. Stuffing the tote they'd knocked heads over under his arm, he picked up her other suitcases and led the way. "You're in number four."

"Oh. Thank you."

He slid a look at her as she caught up with him, baffled by his reaction to her. It was hard to tell what was under her colorful outfit. Her flowered skirt hung loosely almost to her ankles, and even those were hidden by neon orange socks. The green top she wore was baggy, without even a suggestion of womanly curves beneath. Which was fine with him.

Stepping up onto the tiny cabin porch, Trey set down one suitcase to reach for the door. "What's the *M* for?" he asked.

"Um…Margaret."

He opened the door and stepped aside to let her pass into the room. "Friends call you Margie?"

Her throaty chuckle sent shockwaves through him as she stepped past him. He attempted to swallow and found he couldn't.

"No, just Margaret," she answered. "Or Meg. Sometimes."

He managed to clear the thickness from his throat. Still unable to think of a reply, he placed the suitcases inside the door and watched her. Something about the way she moved held his attention.

"It's a very nice cabin," she said from across the room.

Determined to be the kind of cowboy people expected to find on a Texas ranch, Trey touched the brim of his hat and grinned. "Glad you like it, ma'am," he said with an exaggerated drawl. "You might want to jingle your spurs a little. They'll be servin' supper at the chuckwagon any time."

One perfectly arched eyebrow raised in a dark point over one eye. "I guess I wouldn't want to miss that, would I?"

Avoiding her eyes, but with his attention still on her face, Trey noticed her flawless complexion. It didn't go with her mousy hair color at all. Or those fascinating eyes. And her mouth—full lips curved in a slight smile. The thought passed through his mind that it would be mighty nice to have a taste of those lips.

He shook his head at the crazy notion, even as his pulse quickened. *Get a grip, Brannigan.* Taking a backward step out the cabin door, he pulled off his hat, twisting it in his hands. "Well, I'll be leavin' you to…uh…if you need anything…"

"Yes?" she asked in a breathy voice that sped up his heart rate a little more.

"You just ask one of the hands," he finished in a rush, jamming his hat back on his head. Turning, he made for the steps on feet that didn't want to cooperate, and headed across the yard in the direction of the barn.

What the hell was wrong with him? Trey Brannigan tongue-tied? The idea was dumber than a day-old calf. Even his brothers, Dev and Chace, had never been able to render him speechless. Hell, what he needed was a stiff drink. And he'd have one, just as soon as he checked on the status of the stock. He needed to clear his mind and straighten it out again. Women didn't get to him—hadn't in all his thirty-one years. Except once, and that mistake wouldn't happen again. He'd be damned if he knew what had gotten into him now.

Stunned by the cowboy's sudden departure, Meg Chastain moved to the doorway and watched him cross the expanse of well-tended grass between the guest cabins and the ranch's outbuildings. Forcing herself to close the door on the view, she leaned back against it and took a deep breath. This wasn't going to be as easy as she had thought. Merciful heaven! The man moved like his joints were greased with saddle oil, his hips rotating with each step. She'd never get the image out of her mind.

Forcing herself to move, she pushed away from the door and crossed the room, making mental notes of the amenities and ambiance of the cool blue-and-green room. But even in the air-conditioned cabin, an unaccustomed warmth mixed with the heat from her long drive. Fanning herself with one hand, she wondered if she would she ever be cool again. Sweat had glued a curl of hair to her forehead and trickled between her breasts. She blew at the curl but it remained stuck. A quick swipe with the back of her hand moved it away, only to have it dip back down and stick again. Exasperated, she reached for her mop of curls and grabbed a handful, pulling off the wig. Her hair tumbled past her shoulders, damp from the sweat caused by the heat she'd endured during her two and a half day drive.

Men sweat, women perspire, she imagined her Aunt Dee telling her. Meg smiled at the thought. She'd been listening to her aunt's sage advice and quaint sayings for most of her twenty-seven years, and they still never failed to make her smile.

"Sorry, Aunt Dee," she muttered under her breath. "You try driving in this Texas heat in a car with no air-conditioning." If the change in arrangements hadn't been made at the last minute, she would've flown. She was almost two hours late, but at least she'd made it to the Triple B Dude Ranch.

After tossing the glasses she wore only for effect onto the bed, she located the shower and availed herself of its soothing spray. The water did wonders for her aching muscles. But the image of the cowboy popped into her mind again. Those scuffed cowboy boots and worn blue jeans, hugging a pair of muscled thighs, had taken her breath away. The memory of faded chambray draping a pair of broad, solid shoulders still made her catch her breath, while his strong, rugged features and bright blue eyes had almost rendered her speechless.

Her groan filled the small confines of the shower. She knew better than to dwell for even a moment on the fine specimen of pure cowboy maleness that had greeted her on her arrival.

When she finally felt human again, she finished up and dressed. Slipping the wig and glasses on, she checked her reflection in the mirror, smiling at the image staring back at her. No one would pay the least bit of attention to a mousy woman with little knowledge of ranches. Any questions she would ask would seem perfectly normal.

"Now to find Mr. Buford Brannigan." Stepping out into the lengthening shadows of the evening, Meg squared her shoulders and started walking in the direction of the sprawling two-story ranch home.

"You'd better hustle on over for some grub," a slow Texas drawl interrupted her thoughts.

Meg's stomach fluttered at the sound of the deep, smooth baritone, and she turned to see her cowboy walking toward her. *Her* cowboy? She shook her head and silently scolded herself. Considering her reaction, it might be wiser to ask someone else about Buford Brannigan. She'd be smart to keep her distance from this particular cowboy. She wasn't here to get involved with a ranch hand. She was here to do a job.

She noticed a group of people gathered around what appeared to be a covered wagon, and the delicious aroma of barbecue caused her stomach to rumble.

Before she could take a step in that direction, the cowboy approached her, stopping a few feet in front of her. "Hungry, Miss Chastain?"

Was he for real? This was supposed to be a working dude ranch. But could this good-looking hunk, his dark hair curling beneath his gray cowboy hat, be nothing more than a transplant from back east? It wouldn't be the first time dude ranch guests had been fooled.

"The food smells wonderful," she answered.

He looked over his shoulder, then turned back to her. "Looks like there's still a few places to sit."

"Are you joining us?" she asked, praying he wasn't. He was a distraction she didn't need right now.

"Maybe later. I—" He looked down at a little girl of about eight who had appeared at his elbow and was tugging at his shirtsleeve. "Howdy," he said, giving her his attention.

She looked up at him with deep brown eyes that widened. "Are you a real cowboy?"

"Yep."

"Do you ride a horse all day?"

He grinned at her. "Not all day. There's lots of work to do on a ranch besides ridin' horses."

"Like what?"

"Makin' sure the stock's taken care of."

"Stock?"

"You know. Cows, horses. The animals. And we're expectin' some new kittens any day."

"Really?" she asked, her eyes wide. Ducking her head, she scuffed the toe of her shoe in the dirt.

Meg noticed the girl's hesitation and stuck out her

hand. "My name's—" She hesitated for a moment, quickly reminding herself why she was there and who she was supposed to be. "My name's Margaret Chastain, but you can call me Meg. What's yours?"

"Carrie Winston," the little girl answered.

"Do you know how to ride a horse, Carrie?" the cowboy asked.

Carrie shook her head.

"What about you, Miss Chastain?" he asked, turning his attention to her. "Do you like to ride?"

Meg looked up at him. "I—no, not very much."

"Maybe you just need a good teacher."

Meg's breath caught in her throat. It wasn't what he'd said, it was how he'd said it. There was a hint of a promise in his voice and a suggestion of something in his eyes, just before he pulled his hat down, hiding the top half of his face.

"Maybe Carrie can take riding lessons," Meg suggested, forcing herself to breathe again. "They're offered here, aren't they, Mr…?"

"It's Trey, ma'am." He touched the lowered brim of his hat, and she could feel him studying her in the dimming light.

Carrie tugged on his shirtsleeve. "Can I? Can I take riding lessons?"

"Sure you can. I'll let Ellie know." Trey nudged his hat back, grinning at the child, and placed his hand on her shoulder. "Ellie's our riding instructor. Pete, over there, is our head wrangler," he said, nodding in the direction of two men—one of them a cowboy, true to form, the other a tall, lean man in gray slacks and a sports shirt. "Ellie must be busy with the horses. Why don't I mosey on over there and talk to Pete about those lessons? You ready to start in the morning?"

Carrie looked up at Meg, excitement shining in her eyes. "Oh, yes! I have to tell my grandmother!"

As Carrie skipped away, Trey turned to Meg. "How about you, Miss Chastain? Are you interested in lessons?"

Meg hesitated. Ride a horse? The idea made her want to run for the rugged hills that framed the ranch, but she held steady. Riding would be expected of the guests, and she had signed up for the trail ride at the end of the week. Geraldine had insisted on it, even though this entire trip was an effort made in desperation. But Meg didn't care. She needed this. Without it, things wouldn't get better. And they had to.

"I'm game if Carrie is," she finally answered.

"I'll get you both set up, then," he said, with another touch of his hat. He turned to leave, and Meg couldn't stop herself from watching him.

When the cowboy had ambled across the dining area and disappeared, Meg let out her breath in a slow whoosh. As if in reply, her stomach rumbled again, reminding her that she hadn't eaten. There were only a few empty seats left, so she hurried to the chuckwagon to fill a plate. Her late arrival had put her at a disadvantage. She had missed the small welcome party that had been advertised in the ranch's brochure. Besides Carrie, Meg hadn't had a chance to meet any of the other guests. She needed to make up for lost time. Later, during the campfire, she hoped to learn as much as she could about the Triple B Dude Ranch.

But as she took her seat on the bench at the long trestle table set up for the evening meal, she realized she had a direct view of the main ranch house. She could see the cowboy, who was now walking up the steps of the porch, and it was impossible to drag her gaze away. She would have to be careful around him. The way he looked at her, as if he could see beyond her disguise, it wouldn't take long before he guessed the truth. She couldn't risk that. With luck, she would soon be in a better position to help Aunt Dee. Once she had the means to move them to a climate where her aunt's asthma would be better, they could both begin to relax and enjoy life. But that would happen only if she kept her mind on her reason for being here, not on a sexy ranch hand.

After making sure everything was back to normal following the disasters of the morning, Trey stepped off the porch and crossed the yard, his heart swelling with pride at the view. Situated on a rolling field that edged the rugged Banderas terrain, the main buildings glowed golden. The sun's descent toward the horizon offered a breathtaking panorama. A man couldn't ask for much more, except maybe to be a success.

Aromas from the best food south of the Mason-Dixon made his mouth water. Smiling and nodding at guests, he approached the chuckwagon. Satisfied that everything was now running smoothly, he grabbed a plate and filled it, then turned to search for a seat at the long trestle table. But the only spot available was on the end, and directly across from Meg Chastain.

Trey considered carrying his plate to the barn, but it

would only put off the inevitable. He couldn't entirely avoid the woman for a full week. He needed to get accustomed to her green eyes, or discover what it was about her that sent a fog through his mind—and a blaze through his body that he didn't want to acknowledge.

She was talking to a young couple seated on her right when he placed his food on the table and swung first one leg over the bench, then the other. An older woman on his right was deep in conversation with another couple.

"Howdy," he said to no one in particular, picking up his fork. He eyed the tender ribs on his plate, determined that the woman across from him wouldn't get to him this time.

"Hello," she said. "I see you decided to join us after all."

He took a bite of a rib, dripping with barbecue sauce, and looked up—right into Meg Chastain's emerald eyes. He was caught again, and barely noticed the older woman beside him leave the table. All he could do was concentrate on getting past the effect those eyes had on him.

Knowing that conversation was required, he quickly swallowed. "Business. I had some ranch business to take care of."

The woman beside Meg smiled at him. "It's just beautiful here. Ted and I are so impressed. And this food!"

The man next to her nodded. "My hat is off to whoever cooked this wonderful meal."

Trey nearly sighed out loud with relief when Meg's gaze moved to the couple, giving him the chance to clear his head and answer. "That would be Theresa. She's the best." He mentally went through the names of the guests. "Mr. and Mrs. Henderson, right?"

They smiled at each other. "Why, yes, that's right," Mrs. Henderson answered.

But Trey's relief was short-lived when Meg smiled at them. The warmth of it nearly knocked him over. He recovered quickly and was ready when she turned back to him.

"How long has Theresa cooked for the ranch?" she asked.

"Always. We wouldn't want anyone else."

Mr. Henderson stood and helped his wife to her feet as she navigated the table and bench. "I can't blame you for that," he told Trey. "But it wouldn't surprise me if someone tried to steal her away," he added with a chuckle. "With meals like this one, I'll need all the exercise I can get this week. Is it all right if Janet and I take a walk around the place?"

"Please do," Trey said, standing to extend his hand. "And if you need anything, just let any of the staff know. Hope to see you both at the campfire later."

Henderson took the hand Trey offered and shook it. "Thanks. We'll be there."

The couple spoke briefly to Meg, and then walked away, looking satisfied. And leaving Trey alone with the one woman he didn't want to be left alone with. "Nice folks," he said, filling the silence.

"Everyone I've met is very nice. And to echo Janet Henderson, it's beautiful here."

"I'd be a fool to disagree with that," he replied with a grin.

Falling silent while they both finished their meal, Trey did his best to focus on the plate of food before him. But he couldn't stop himself from glancing at his supper companion from time to time, trying to figure out what kind of woman she was. He divided women into two types. The first included the ones with dynamite curves, who were out for a good time. They were the women he felt most comfortable with, because the second kind was the settlin' down type. He enjoyed his freedom too much to get caught up with one of them. Not that he didn't like them, but he had learned it always led to someone getting hurt. The first type understood him. The second type wanted to tie him down. Meg had him baffled as to where she fit. But it didn't really matter. He didn't have time for a woman right now. Either kind. And even if he did, he'd let his brother, Chace, be the one to enjoy married life. Trey liked his own footloose and fancy-free.

Rolling his napkin into a ball when his plate was empty, he prepared to leave, wondering what he should say to the woman across the table from him. The things he wanted to say—the things he normally said to a woman he was attracted to—were on the tip of his tongue. Lucky for him, that was pretty much still tied in a knot.

While he continued to watch her, Meg carefully placed her utensils on her plate and touched her napkin to her mouth. "When did the ranch open for business?"

He tore his gaze away from the simple movement and concentrated on her left earlobe, where he felt fairly safe. "Eight months ago, in December last year."

"Is it cold here in the winter?"

"Pretty mild. It gets cool, but not downright cold.

How about yours?" he asked, wondering where she hailed from.

"Cold," she said with a wry smile. "Very cold."

"You're from back east?"

She shook her head. "More like up north, with lots of ice and snow. I wouldn't know it was winter without it."

When she looked at him again, their gazes locked, and she blushed. Staring into her eyes, even for a moment, left him breathless.

"Well," she said, standing and gathering her supper things, "I guess I need to get unpacked. Thank you for keeping me company."

He felt both relieved and bereft when she looked away. "Let me take care of that." He stood and took the plate from her, adding his own. "Don't forget the campfire, in about an hour," he said, touching the brim of his hat and turning to leave.

As he walked away, he could feel her watching him. It wasn't something he was unfamiliar with. Women usually liked him as much as he noticed them. But this time, it felt different somehow. Exactly how, he couldn't say. Just...different.

He shook off the sensation and strode with purpose to dispose of the remnants of their supper, determined to end the day better than it had started. He'd had nothing but bad news since early that morning, when his two best ranch hands had gotten themselves run down by the new Brahma bull. The animal was now loose in the south pasture, along with the dozen and a half calves who'd managed to escape *their* pen. Because of that, he'd been doing double duty, welcoming guests to the

Triple B Dude Ranch and covering for his injured men. And if all that wasn't bad enough, the ranch's secretary hadn't shown up for work...again. It was understandable that he was exhausted. Maybe that explained his foggy-headed feeling.

There were more important things to be thinking about than a woman with a pair of devastating green eyes that seemed to see inside him, clear down to his soul. There was the Triple B. That's where his heart was. It was the most important thing in his life. And it always would be.

Chapter Two

Meg chose one of the many bales of hay surrounding the campfire, making certain she had a clear view of everyone and everything, and settled onto it. Wincing, she shifted position, trying to find a spot where the sharp straw didn't poke through the thin cotton of her skirt. She had packed a few pairs of jeans, just in case, but had hoped she wouldn't have to wear them. They didn't hide her figure—a figure she found a nuisance. But when it came to the riding lessons she had agreed to take, there wasn't any way she could get away with wearing one of the hideous skirts she'd brought with her.

Eventually finding a comfortable spot, she greeted the woman sitting next to her. As they chatted about the ranch and how much they were enjoying it, a shadow blocked the light from the campfire.

Meg looked up to see Trey standing in front of her,

the glow from the firelight behind him setting off his silhouette. With his thumbs hooked into his belt, and his cowboy hat tipped back on his head, Meg couldn't help but be impressed by the figure he cut. Strong broad shoulders and a wide chest narrowed to hips and muscled thighs beneath denim. It was a sight that would take any woman's breath away. It definitely took Meg's.

"Havin' a good time?" he asked.

Before Meg could find enough breath to answer, Carrie appeared and tugged at his shirt. "We're going to have our riding lesson in the morning, aren't we?"

His deep laughter sent warm shivers up and down Meg's spine. He placed a hand on top of Carrie's head. "First thing in the mornin' after breakfast. I already have a horse picked out especially for you."

"Really?"

He looked at Meg, the firelight dancing behind him. After what seemed like several minutes had gone by, he dragged his gaze away and reached down to tap the little girl's nose with one finger. "Really."

Carrie squealed with delight, but Meg couldn't stop looking at the cowboy whose attention was now elsewhere.

He backed up a step and nodded, tugging his hat down and touching two fingers to the wide brim. "See you at breakfast," he said without looking at Meg.

Carrie spun around to face her. "Do you think it'll be a fast horse?"

Reluctantly pulling her attention from the fascinating sight of the retreating backside of the cowboy, Meg squelched a sigh before answering. Her heartbeat had picked up since he'd walked up to them and now raced in double-time.

"Not *too* fast," she answered. But whether her answer was directed at Carrie or a command to her own galloping heart, she wasn't sure.

Nodding, Carrie covered a yawn with her hand, and Meg stood. Taking the child by the hand, she gave her a friendly squeeze. "Let's find your grandmother so she can get you into bed. You'll need some sleep if you're going to learn to ride a horse tomorrow."

Carrie looked up at her. "But nobody else is going to bed."

"I am," Meg answered.

It didn't take long for them to find Carrie's grandmother. After a brief discussion of the plans for the next day, Meg bade them good-night and started for her cabin.

The air around her was pure and clean, so different from the city air where she lived. Breathing deeply, she tipped her head up and gazed at the canopy of stars above her. She couldn't remember ever having seen anything quite so beautiful. Someday, she and her aunt would be able to enjoy the same kind of beauty. That's why it was so important that she keep her mind on the reason she was here, not on a sexy ranch hand who she'd never see again after the week was over.

Movement in the darkness to her left brought her to a halt. Her heart beat harder and fear prickled her skin. "Is someone there?" she asked, her voice sounding weaker than she had hoped.

"Didn't mean to scare you."

She instantly recognized Trey's drawl and breathed

easier. "Oh! It's you." Much to her disgust, the beating of her heart didn't slow down at all.

He caught up with her, shortening his long stride to match hers when she continued walking. "You're turnin' in early."

She glanced up to see him watching her. "It was a long drive, and since I'll need to be clear-headed for the riding lesson in the morning, I thought I should get some sleep."

"Where did you say you're from?"

"I didn't," she admitted, with a smile. "But Indiana is home."

He let out a long whistle. "That *is* a long drive."

"I enjoyed it," she admitted. "Except for the heat. But it's the first time I've ever had the opportunity to see much of the country."

"I saw enough of it when I was rodeoing, and this is still the best."

The pride in his voice was obvious. She couldn't blame him. The ranch and the countryside surrounding it were breathtaking. "What did you do in the rodeo?"

He was so close, she felt his shrug. "A little this, a little that. Mostly saddle bronc riding."

"I've never been to a rodeo, but I've watched them on TV. To be honest, they're frightening. Isn't it terribly dangerous on those horses?"

"Lots of injuries, but if it's in your blood, those don't matter. My brother was a double National Champion the last year he competed, so I guess you could say it's in his blood. Not really in mine, though," he added with a soft chuckle. "Give me ranching, any day."

Neither of them spoke again until they neared her cabin. Meg wondered what he was thinking about, but didn't ask. The silence between them was comfortable and she didn't feel the need for conversation.

As they reached the porch, Trey slowed his steps. "I'd better get back to work."

In spite of knowing she shouldn't, Meg was sorry to see him go. "And I need to get that sleep."

They stood staring at one another in the darkness. Finally, Trey cleared his throat. "See you at breakfast. Sleep tight."

Meg thanked him for keeping her company once again, then slipped into her cabin. Before she closed the door, she searched for a glimpse of him, but couldn't see much of anything.

"Just as well," she whispered to herself. Tomorrow would arrive soon enough, and she would have to get to work. She had learned more about Trey than she had about the ranch, and even though she enjoyed his company, she had to get some sleep. And she still needed to find Buford Brannigan.

"What do you mean, you're not teaching the class?" Trey boomed down at his pint-size sister-in-law early the next morning.

Ellie Brannigan leaned back against the corral fence, crossing her arms on her chest. "Calm down, Trey. We're short-handed, remember? And Sherry called this morning to say she wouldn't be in again today. Somebody's got to hang around the office to answer the phone and get the paperwork caught up. I'm the likely candidate."

"But who's going to teach the riding class?"

"Why, you are," she said, pushing off and starting for the big double barn door.

Trey grabbed her arm before she could take two steps. "Wait a minute. Why me?"

Pulling away from him, she planted her hands on her hips and tipped up her head to look at him. "Because you can't spare any of the other hands, that's why. And you know as much about horses and riding as I do."

She was right, but the last thing he needed was to spend more time around Meg Chastain. When he'd left her at her cabin last night he'd made the decision to put as much distance between himself and the green-eyed woman as possible. Teaching the riding lesson would throw them together again. Exactly what he didn't need.

"I can't do it," he said, dragging his hat from his head and raking a hand through his hair.

"Oh, puh-leeze."

"No, really," he argued, jamming his hat back on his head. How was he supposed to tell her that his plans for the day didn't include being around Meg? For some reason, Meg was worming her way into his mind. There was something about her that he couldn't explain—especially not to his brother's wife.

"Look, I'll go get the paperwork done while you teach the riding lesson," he said with hope.

"You don't have a clue where anything is," Ellie reminded him.

Trey hated to admit she was right. He might do the majority of the business end of the ranch work, but he was about as organized as a drowning man. If it weren't for their young secretary, the Triple B would be in bad shape. He could handle the simple stuff—keeping stock records, ordering feed and the "dude" part of the ranch. But when it came to the other paperwork, he needed help.

"Okay," he relented. "But just for today, you got that? When Sherry gets back tomorrow, I'm off the hook and you're back with the lessons."

Patting his shoulder, Ellie smiled. "She said she had some personal business to take care of today. Things should be back to normal tomorrow."

"Nothing will be normal," he grumbled as she walked away. He didn't bother to return the grin she gave him over her shoulder.

A sigh of frustration ended his self-pity. He had a choice. Go with the flow and deal with the catastrophes that seemed to be plaguing him this week, or give up. And he wasn't about to give up. There was too much at stake. The Triple B wasn't only his livelihood. It was Ellie's and Chace's, too. Trey knew his brother was eager to start a family to carry on the Brannigan name, but neither Chace nor Ellie wanted to put a strain on things until they were certain the dude ranch was going to be profitable. Until they could regularly draw in larger groups, like the one this week, that wouldn't happen.

With a kick at a dirt clod, Trey headed for the large, modern horse barn. He had a vague idea who would be riding and what horse each guest would use, but he needed to make sure all was in order before the group descended on him.

Once inside, he stopped at the first stall to check on the gentle pinto mare he'd chosen for Carrie. Satisfied with his choice, he moved on to check the other horses. Everything had to be perfect. The welfare of his guests was top priority. He couldn't risk having one of them land on his or her butt and go screaming "lawsuit" all the way back to whatever city they'd come from. The Triple B couldn't afford anything like that.

A whinny from a stall farther down caught his attention. Turning, Trey saw the bay gelding shaking its head as if in answer to a disturbing question. Concerned there might be a varmint in the enclosed area with the horse, Trey moved down the walkway and silently peeked into the stall. He expected to see anything from a small mouse to a polecat, but what he saw made him freeze.

Meg Chastain knelt in the corner, her back to him, whispering comfort to something. Trey hoped to hell it wasn't something that could hurt her. An armadillo wasn't a pretty sight, nor was a possum, but there was no accounting for some people's soft spots.

When he saw the silver-gray of the mother cat rubbing against Meg's leg, he relaxed. Crossing his arms on the gate in front of him, he watched her. The gelding moved closer to Trey, who absentmindedly scratched between the horse's ears. He knew that if either he or the horse made any sudden moves, they'd scare the daylights out of the woman. He sure didn't want that to happen. Besides, he didn't want to lose this opportunity to take a close look at her while her attention was somewhere else. Maybe he could figure out what it was about her that had his curiosity and his pulse at a high.

He couldn't see much of her. Like she had the day

before, she was wearing a big, tent-like top that hid whatever she had under it. The way she was kneeling made the bottom of it hang around her, shrouding her and covering whatever she had on from the waist down. He couldn't tell what that was, but a hint of denim winked at the tops of her hot pink tennis shoes.

Taking his time, his gaze wandered up her back and stopped at the slender column of her neck. With her head tipped forward, the creamy ivory of her revealed skin beckoned to him, silently begging for his lips to press against it. He warmed to the idea, almost ready to move in her direction to do the deed. Reaching out for the gate latch, he froze and shook his head. What the hell was he doing?

Meg twisted to look over her shoulder, ruining the view he'd had of her bared neck. Trey swallowed as his gaze slid to hers. Behind her round lenses, her eyes were wide with surprise, pulling him deeper into their cool, green depths.

She turned, breaking the spell, and he let out a whoosh of air. Pulling himself together, he silently cursed himself for letting her get to him. By the time she turned around again, he was ready for those killer eyes.

"Kittens," she said, holding up a tiny ball of slightly damp fur against one flushed cheek. "Carrie will love these."

He nodded. "Too bad they won't be big enough for her to take one home."

Meg answered with a knowing smile and turned back to return the kitten. She slowly got to her feet and faced him, brushing off clinging bits of straw. "I hope the barn isn't off-limits."

Jeans, he thought, running his gaze quickly over the bottom half of her legs. But that's all he could see. The long top covered everything from just above her knees on up. Below that, he could only guess at what was suggested.

"Is it?" she asked.

"What?" He looked into her emerald eyes and felt like a mule had kicked him in the chest. It took him a moment to regain his equilibrium, and he forced himself to look away before he lost what little control he had left. Stepping back from the stall, he stuffed his hands in his pockets, hoping to look unaffected.

"Is the barn off-limits?" she asked. "I'd like to show Carrie the kittens after our riding lesson."

"No," he replied with a shake of his head. "I mean, it's okay. Just make sure she's careful around Pedro, there." He inclined his head towards the horse that had moved away to the far corner. "I'm surprised you're in the stall with him."

Sudden realization and fear sparkled in her eyes. "Is he dangerous?"

"He's fairly gentle. I reckon he didn't sense any fear in you."

"I-I wasn't paying attention. I didn't even notice him. I heard the kittens mewing and I—" Her cheeks were pale as she pressed against the side of the stall and eased along it, keeping her attention on the horse. "Maybe I'd better— I guess it's about time for the lesson to start. I'd better get Carrie so we won't be late."

He opened the gate and held it for her. Unfortunately, he got a whiff of her as she passed. Soft, sweet, gentle as a summer evening, her scent drew him in. Managing to keep his feet planted, he could only nod in answer.

"I'll see you around, I guess," she said, squaring her shoulders and turning to leave.

Trey suddenly remembered that *he* would be teaching the class, not Ellie. He cleared his throat and found his voice. "I'll be teaching the riding today."

She came to a stop halfway to the wide double doors and looked back at him, her features troubled. "I thought you said somebody named Ellie would be teaching it."

"Yeah, well…" He shrugged. Hoping she'd change her mind about going ahead with the class, he waited.

Indecision danced around her well-covered body. "Well, I can't let Carrie down," she said, more to herself than to him. With a shrug of her own, she hurried from the barn.

Damn. Looked like he didn't have a choice. He'd be teaching her how to ride. She didn't seem to have any sense about how to act around horses, but he crossed his fingers and hoped she'd get the hang of riding quickly. He wasn't sure how much time he dared spend around her. And if he was smart, he'd stop encouraging her. The only way he could do that was not to talk to her unless absolutely necessary. Damn his bad luck.

Trey stood near the doors of the stable, his hat pulled low, blocking the morning sun that bathed his tanned face. "Come on in the barn and I'll show y'all how to dress out a horse."

Joining the other four guests as they followed Trey into the barn for their riding lesson, Meg bit her lip to keep her nervous giggle at bay. Would the animals be wearing career clothes? After all, this was their job. Or would they be dressed in casual wear?

Inside the barn, Meg stood, fascinated, as she watched Trey instruct them on the fine art of saddling a horse. His expert and graceful movements held her attention as he slowly went through each and every step of readying a horse for riding. His strong hands were long-fingered, tanned and callused, but gentle in their movements. When Meg realized she was wondering what those hands would feel like caressing her body, she put the brakes on her wayward thoughts. Oh, no, she wasn't going to let herself be taken in. This cowboy was a ranch hand, and although he might be useful to her, there would be nothing more. Besides, he was probably like all the other men she had met. He might look gentle, but more than likely it was pure deception.

"Okay," Trey said, bringing Meg out of her reverie. "I'll assign y'all each a horse, and then I want to see you do it. I'll give you a hand if you need help."

Meg shuddered, her nerves giving way to pure terror. If Trey hadn't found her in the stall earlier with the kittens, she wondered how she would've gotten out. Growing up in Gary, Indiana, hadn't lent itself to riding horses. She barely knew the front end from the back end. Now she was going to have to climb on one.

Meg felt a small hand slip into hers, and she looked down to see Carrie.

"I don't think I can lift the saddle," the little girl said, her voice wobbling.

Before Meg could think of something to say to reassure her, Trey joined them and bent down to Carrie's eye level. "Don't worry about it, sweetheart. Nobody expects you to. Soon as I help Miss Chastain, I'll get you all ready to ride." He straightened and looked directly at Meg.

She hated to admit that the thought of saddling a horse had her scared witless. "Just show me the horse," she announced, hoping her voice wasn't as shaky as her knees were.

Sliding her a strange look, Trey shrugged. "Sure you can lift that saddle?"

She flashed him what she hoped was a confident smile. "I'm much stronger than I look. Go ahead and help Carrie. I'll let you know if I need help."

With a nod, he pointed to a nearby stall. "See that palomino? He's yours."

Her breath caught at the sight of the beautiful horse, and she hoped that she wouldn't be afraid of such a gorgeous animal. "Does he have a name?"

"Moonlight. And he's gentle, so don't let him spook you if he starts moving around."

With her knees feeling like rubber, she took the few steps and reached the stall. Easing into it, where the palomino stood waiting, she kept her voice low and much calmer than she felt. "Hey, Moonlight, I'm Meg. And aren't you a beauty?" Her hand trembled as she tentatively reached up to comb her fingers through his mane. Taking a deep breath, she stepped back. "I'm going to saddle you now," she warned.

She lifted the saddle from the top of the half-wall between stalls, and the weight of it nearly buckled her knees, forcing her to lean against the stall to stay upright. But she was determined to do this herself.

The horse, as beautiful as he was, wouldn't cooperate. Each time Meg hefted the saddle higher, he sidestepped. She cursed him under her breath, determined that one way or another she was going to get it done. Gripping the leather and taking a fortifying breath, she tried once more. The horse backed away, his ears pressed flat to his head, and he snorted. Meg jumped back at the unusual sound, lost her balance, and the weight of the saddle brought her to the ground with an *oomph* of air. Tears of frustration burned her eyes.

"Problems?"

She jerked her head around at the sound of Trey's voice and looked up to find him watching her. She sniffed at the tears and shrugged. "Maybe I'm not as strong as I thought I was."

He opened the gate and walked in, his attention on the saddle holding her to the straw-covered floor. "You okay?" he asked as he lifted the saddle off her.

She scrambled to her feet, dusting off her backside and picking off bits of clinging straw. "I'm fine," she answered, stepping back to give him plenty of room in the stall. *Except for my dignity.*

His gaze raked her from head to foot, then he shook his head. "You forgot the saddle blanket." Picking up the brightly colored woven cloth, he proceeded to saddle the horse. "Pay close attention. Next time you'll get it right."

"It seems to me it makes more sense to use a blanket when he goes to bed."

His hands stilled on the buckle he was tightening and

he made a choking sound. "Horses don't sleep under blankets, as a rule." When he finished, he spun around and left her standing alone in the stall. "Let's all get out to the corral," he called to the others.

Leading her own saddled horse, Carrie patted Meg's arm. "Don't feel bad. I couldn't do it either."

"Right," Meg answered, forcing a grin. She did a quick once-over of Carrie and her horse, finally realizing that she needed to loop the long strip of leather connected to the things in the horse's mouth over the horse's neck before she could lead him. She definitely had a lot to learn.

Outside, in the corral, Trey held a stunning black horse and demonstrated the proper method of mounting. "From the left side," he was explaining, "grip the saddle horn with your left hand and the back of the cantle with your right. Put your left foot in the stirrup, and then swing your right leg over, like this." With a grace that belied his size, Trey swung into the saddle. "Keep your heels down, knees hugging the horse, hand firmly gripping the reins. But don't pull. These are like the steering wheel and brakes on your car, only more so. You think power steering and brakes are touchy? It's nothin' compared to these animals."

Meg helped Carrie, doing her best to hold the horse steady beneath the child. But her attention was on Trey and the fine figure he cut atop the horse. The way they moved as one around the fenced area was pure artistry, and she suddenly understood the saying about someone looking like he'd been born in the saddle.

And now it was her turn to climb on Moonlight. The thought scared her to death.

Once Carrie was settled in the saddle, Meg started behind the little black and white horse and felt herself being jerked away, the grip on her forearm causing her to wince.

"Are you crazy, woman? Not behind the horse," Trey growled. "You want to get your teeth kicked out?"

"Why would he do that?"

Trey stared at her, then shook his head. "*She* can't see you back there." He kept his grip on Meg and led her to the palomino. "Let me see you mount."

As they approached the horse, Meg swallowed the lump of fear in her throat. With more than a little trepidation, she lifted a foot into the stirrup.

Grabbing her calf, Trey eased her leg down to the ground. "*Left* side, *left* foot."

She looked at him and then at the horse. "Right," she said, nodding, and forced a smile. A giggle bubbled in her throat. "I mean *left*, and *you're* right. Um, correct."

Starting around the back of the horse, she halted. "See? I remember," she said, flashing him a grin before retracing her steps to go the other way. On the left side, she lifted her left foot to the stirrup, glancing over the horse's back at the man watching her. Flashing him a shaky smile, she jumped but landed with her right foot still on the ground. Then jumped again. Then again, getting absolutely nowhere.

"Put your weight on the foot in the stirrup and *swing* your other leg over the horse," Trey said, walking around the horse. Bending down, he grasped her calf. "Now try it."

She nearly fell into her instructor when he pressed his

hand to her bottom. As he boosted her up, she came close to sailing over the top of the horse, and had to grab the saddle horn to keep from toppling over onto the ground.

"Thanks," she said, gritting her teeth and attempting a smile.

"You okay?" he asked, settling his hand on her thigh.

Meg gulped at the heat his touch sent spiraling through her. Looking down, she stared at his hand. "Um, yeah," she answered, her voice barely a whisper.

As if he had just noticed he was touching her, he jerked back and spun around so fast, it nearly made her dizzy. Mounting his own horse, he called to the others. "Listen up, folks. Give the reins a little flick," he said, demonstrating with a quick movement of his wrist, "then touch—and I do mean touch—your heels to the horse's side. Once you get moving, just circle around."

Forcing her racing heart to calm, Meg concentrated on the idea of actually riding the horse and did as he'd instructed, but the horse didn't budge. She tried pulling the reins, but still no luck. When Moonlight didn't respond, she tried the last thing she could think of. "Move horse," she said, throwing her upper body forward in the saddle. To her surprise, the horse began to walk.

"Knees in, Miss Chastain," Trey ordered from across the corral. "And get those heels down. Without boots, you could get your ankle busted real easy if you don't."

Meg quickly complied. The last thing she needed was to be laid up with a broken bone. An accident would take her out of the ranch activities, and she needed to be in the thick of things.

Trey approached her and brought his horse to a stop.

"Maybe you oughta go into San Antonio and get yourself a pair of boots. If you're plannin' on doin' anymore ridin', that is."

"I'll do that." she answered as he turned to ride away. She wasn't at all convinced she would ever do this again.

With a sigh of relief when Trey called the group's riding to a halt, Meg started to dismount, only to find a pair of strong hands grasping her hips. The sigh instantly became a gasp as she was lowered to the ground. Once her feet were firmly planted in the dirt, she turned to see Trey, his blue eyes wide, as if he were surprised.

He released her and shook his head, backing up a step. "Didn't want you to fall, considerin' the trouble you had gettin' on."

Meg bit down on her lip, refusing to acknowledge the sparks skipping through her body. Between the way his touch affected her and her insecurity on a horse, she wondered how she would last the week. She had been crazy to agree to come here, but there wasn't much she could do about it except give it her best shot. And she would. She only hoped it would be good enough.

Chapter Three

Trey watched Meg lead Moonlight into the barn, hypnotized by the seductive movement of her body. Although she was well-covered from chin to toes, there was something so downright sensual in the sway of her hips that he had to hold himself back from following her.

She was hiding under those clothes. She had to be. When he had lifted her down from the horse, his fingers had pressed into a pair of rounded hips. No extra padding there, just sheer woman. He could only wonder at other parts of her—which led him to wonder even more about the kind of woman she really was. That scared him.

"How'd the lessons go?"

Glancing back over his shoulder, he saw his sister-in-law walking toward him. He liked Ellie. Chace couldn't have found a better woman. But Trey wasn't the settlin' down type. There were too many little darlin's to meet and get to know. Meg Chastain was new to him. That must be why he was so intrigued by her. It would wear off, in time. He was sure of it.

With a final quick look in the direction of the barn where Meg had disappeared, Trey forced the memory of the delightful feel of her to a corner of his mind before meeting his brother's wife at the corral fence.

"Lessons weren't too bad," he answered Ellie. "There were only five of 'em. Maybe the rest heard I'd be teaching instead of you," he added with a grin.

Ellie laughed and propped a foot on the bottom fence rail. "Maybe that's it. Anything special I should know? Any problems?"

He thought of Carrie. And Meg. "No problems, but if the little girl plans to go on the trail ride, she might need a little extra attention. A private lesson or two should do it."

"Private lessons are extra," she reminded him.

"Check with her grandmother. I don't think there'll be a problem."

"Anything else?"

But his attention wasn't on her or what she was saying. He watched as Meg strolled out of the barn and crossed the far end of the corral, headed for the guest cabins. He couldn't keep his gaze from zeroing in on the woman, and he let out a breath of air when she disappeared around the corner of the barn.

"How'd she do with the lesson?" Ellie asked, gesturing in Meg's direction.

Trey couldn't deny that Meg was definitely shaky on a horse, but he suspected she would get over it as soon as she understood the basics. "She's doing okay," he hedged, feeling Ellie watching him closely.

"Maybe you'd better find some time for some private lessons with her."

"Me?" he asked, matching her stare for stare. "Where am I supposed to find the time?"

"Oh, like I have the time," she countered, her words dripping with sarcasm. "But you know that if she's having some problems now, they'll be even worse on the trail ride. Better give it some thought."

He shook his head. He'd be damned if he was going to spend any more time with Meg unless he didn't have a choice. "Nope. Not on your life. A couple more group lessons and she'll be fine."

"Yeah, but will you?" Moving away from the fence, she started for the house. "I've got work waiting."

"Ellie," he called to her, determined to put Meg out of his mind. "Chace oughta be back this evening. Has he called?"

"No, not today, but I expect him to later, once he's on the road," she told him over her shoulder.

He nodded as she hurried on to the house. His brother had left early the morning before to drive to Lubbock for their new riding horses. Chace had called when he'd reached the motel last night, and Ellie had relayed the message that all was well and he didn't expect any problems getting the horses or transporting them back to the ranch. One less worry for Trey. And more time to wonder about Meg Chastain's hidden curves and what else she might be hiding. She presented a challenge to him, and he'd be damned if he'd turn it down.

* * *

Meg stepped out onto the small cabin porch and took a deep breath. The scent of ranch permeated the air. She hadn't expected to like it, but she did. The smell of hay and fresh, smog-free air tickled her senses, so different from life in the city. This was what she wanted for Aunt Dee. Clean air. She'd researched several areas of the country, and Arizona always came up. There, allergies would hopefully be a thing of the past, and her aunt would be able to enjoy life, instead of gasping for every breath.

Aunt Dee had never had much. Her health problems had taken any extra money they might have had. Meg wanted to repay her for all the love her aunt had unselfishly given her.

As she made her way to the green meadow behind the cottages and main house, the dry grass whispered against the denim of her jeans while colorful wildflowers caught her eye. Silence surrounded her. Silence of the nicest kind. If she strained her ears, she could hear indistinct voices coming from the ranch proper, but they were nothing compared to the din of the city. She would remember to thank Geraldine, not only for the chance to make a name for herself, but for the opportunity to experience this beautiful part of the country.

Feeling better than she had in a long time, and with her determination to succeed at an all-time high, Meg turned back for the ranch. The sight of a cowboy strolling toward her brought her to a halt. There was no mistaking that easy lope. Her heartbeat immediately picked up, and she took several deep breaths to try to slow it before he reached her. She *had* to get control of herself.

"Havin' trouble findin' somethin' to do?" Trey asked, stopping less than a foot in front of her.

She shook her head. "Just enjoying the great outdoors."

His eyes narrowed against the glow of the setting sun lighting his face. "You aren't gettin' bored at the Triple B, are you?"

"No," she said after a slight hesitation. Was this a good time to ask more questions? Would this cowboy know anything? It was worth a try to find out. "How long have you lived here?"

His slow grin sent her heart rate up another ten beats. With Trey around, she didn't need aerobics. Just his sexy smile.

Tipping his hat farther down and shading his eyes, he chuckled. "Just about forever. And that's about how long it'll be before I leave. What do you think of the place?"

"It's beautiful," she answered truthfully.

"Ever been to Texas before?"

She shook her head. Even with his eyes hidden, she could feel him looking at her. She didn't dare glance at him for more than a minute. His strong but finely chiseled features were enough to make most women she knew swoon. But she wasn't most women. She'd had enough disappointing encounters with men and had decided she could live without them. A career was more lucrative and satisfying. Most men left her feeling cold. To her surprise, Trey didn't. It was startling to be near a man who made the air around her warmer but far from uncomfortable.

But she shouldn't be thinking about him or any man,

she reminded herself. "Didn't I hear the ranch is family-owned?"

Trey barely heard her. He couldn't stop looking at her. Nodding, he lifted his hand to skim a finger down her cheek. Her peaches-and-cream skin was even softer than he'd imagined. And he'd imagined plenty on the drive back from visiting his injured ranch hands in San Antonio that afternoon. "You don't get out in the sun much, do you?" he asked in a voice so husky, it surprised even him.

She cleared her throat before answering, but she didn't move. "N-no," she said, her voice a soft whisper.

He couldn't stop his smile. He was definitely getting to her. But it was *his* heart that skipped a beat. He noticed her quickened breathing and stepped closer, her wide, green eyes drawing him in. A voice in the back of his mind told him this was no way to act with a guest, but he couldn't make himself back off. In spite of the long, loose top she wore, hiding who knew what, the lady had a magnetism. Her delicate features blew his mind. He was accustomed to beautiful woman, but she took his breath away. Her eyes shimmered with apprehension, but he could see a flame of something flickering there, too.

His gaze dropped to her lips. Full and ripe like fresh strawberries, they begged to be tasted. His body responded to the sight of them. Unable to stop himself, he moved his hand to the slender column of her neck, his fingers curving around it while his thumb rested at the base of her throat, where her pulse throbbed beneath his touch.

Lowering his head to answer the silent plea of her lips, he was brought to a halt mere inches from his goal by the sound of a honking horn. She jerked away at the intrusion, and he lost the moment. Silently swearing at himself for his damned fool libido, he dropped his hand and looked down the long drive to see the Triple B pickup and trailer spewing dust as it neared the barn.

"Chace is back," he muttered.

"Chace?"

Trey nodded and moved away from her, watching his brother's progress. "New riding horses," he said and turned back to grin at her. "But you can still ride Moonlight."

"Oh, well, thanks," Meg stammered. "I guess."

"You'll catch up on your ridin' soon. Ellie'll be teachin' from now on." At least he hoped so. If she didn't, he wasn't sure he could keep his attention on ranch business, like he needed to.

"I'd better go help unload," he told Meg.

"Of course," she said. "I mean, after all, that *is* your job. Not…talking to me."

"Even a wrangler gets some down time," he said with a chuckle.

Because the guest cabins were ahead and to their left, and he was headed to the barn on the right, he touched his hat and bid her goodbye. "Don't forget the campfire tonight," he reminded her as he enjoyed the view of her walking away from him. He could have sworn he saw her stumble, and he grinned. He really was getting to her. But why did he want to? He'd sworn to stay away from her. Instead, when he had seen her headed out here, he'd followed her. Why?

Shaking his head at the crazy way he had been acting, Trey hurried to meet Chace at the back of the horse trailer. "Any trouble?"

Chace shot him a smile as he opened the trailer door. "Nope."

Letting out a long breath, Trey nodded. "Maybe things are looking up."

"Looking up? Something wrong? Other than the Brahma accident, that is." Chace shook his head. "Ellie told me about it. That sure puts a crunch on things. More work for you. But you seem to be enjoying it." He jabbed an elbow at Trey's ribs, then eased into the trailer.

"What's that supposed to mean?" Trey hollered at him, stepping out of the way of the horse Chace backed out of the gate.

When he was out in the open again, Chace nodded to the area Trey had just come from. "I saw you out there, little brother. Adding another filly to your stable?"

Trey opened his mouth to deny anything was going on, but closed it. Denial would only set Chace to laughing. "Can't let my charm go to waste," he said with a shrug. "There was a time you could've taken lessons."

"Don't need 'em." Glancing in the direction of the house, Chace grinned. "I did fine without your help."

"You just got lucky and found the right woman," Trey answered. "I'd rather put all my luck into this ranch than into something as skittish as a female."

Giving Trey a brotherly punch on his arm, Chace moved past him, leading the horse. "You just haven't found the right one."

Trey's answer was a snort of laughter. "Maybe I've

just found too many right ones. But look at it this way. If I concentrate on the ranch, and we start seeing some real money, you and Ellie won't have to just talk about starting a family."

"Don't worry about that," Chace called over his shoulder as he entered the barn. "We've been getting in plenty of practice."

Trey looked up to see three of the ranch hands enter the barn. "Help's arrived."

With the extra men to lend a hand, the new horses were unloaded and led to stalls in a short time. When they were finished, Chace handed Trey the bill of sale. It took only a glance at it for Trey to know they had overstepped their budget.

"Yeah, it was a little steeper than we'd planned," Chace said, echoing Trey's thoughts. "But I still have most of the purse from National Finals in savings. I'll make up the difference."

"No," Trey answered, folding the paper and stuffing it into his shirt pocket. "I told you when you agreed to come into this with me that your rodeo winnings weren't going to subsidize the dude part of the ranch." Still, he wasn't sure they could make ends meet, the way he had planned.

"But I was the one who made the decision to spend the extra," Chace insisted.

"A deal's a deal, big brother," Trey reminded him, hoping it would end any more of Chace's arguments. "And I'd better get this entered in the books," he added, patting his pocket. "With Sherry gone, it might get misplaced. We don't need that kind of bookkeeping disaster."

He turned and started for the house. He had some thinking to do. And he needed to stay away from Meg. If it hadn't been for Chace arriving when he had… Trey shook his head. He needed to forget about it. She'd be leaving at the end of the week, and he'd forget her. It was a waste of precious time to keep letting his hormones get the best of him when he had the future of the ranch at stake.

Meg watched out the cabin window until she saw Trey walking in the direction of the ranch house. Scrambling to her feet, she winced at the pain radiating from her backside. The riding lesson had taught her even more than learning to ride. Now she knew that riding a horse was dangerous to delicate body parts, too. After returning to her room to think about what had almost happened with Trey during her walk, she had learned the true meaning of the term "saddle sore." And she had come to a conclusion about what she needed to do.

Once she was out the door and moving, she felt a little better and managed to reach the porch of the house at the same time he did. "Do you have a minute?" she asked.

"Sure. A minute, an hour, as much time as you need."

She chose to forget about their earlier encounter and get right to the decision she had made. "About the trail ride on Saturday," she began, hoping she wasn't making another mistake. She was certain her first had been in being so determined to show him that she would learn to ride. "Well, I signed up for it."

He leaned back against the house and crossed his arms on his chest. His lips twitched in the beginning of a smile. "Good. I can guarantee you'll enjoy it."

"Money back?" she asked, unable to resist.

The hint of a smile he'd worn disappeared for a split second, and then he grinned. "I doubt it'll come to that."

She took a deep breath. "Actually, I want to take my name off the list," she blurted, before she could change her mind.

For a moment, he studied her, and she wished she could just turn around and forget the whole thing. Home sounded good. Their encounter in the grassy field had left her with feelings she didn't want to deal with. Feelings she shouldn't and didn't want to be feeling. They confused her. And frightened her.

"Why don't you have a seat?" he offered, pointing behind her.

She turned to see an old-fashioned porch swing and was tempted. There was a swing similar to it that hung on her aunt's porch in Gary, and Meg had spent half of her lifetime in it, even during snowstorms. But the idea of sitting on anything at the moment was beyond imagining.

"Thank you, but I'll stand," she answered, turning back to look at him.

He fought a definite grin. Then a deep chuckle rumbled in his chest. Before she knew it, he was laughing.

"Happens to everybody," he said, reducing the laughter to a wide, knowing grin. Walking past her to the swing, he picked up a pillow from the floor of the porch. She watched as he dusted it off and plumped it, then placed it on the seat of the swing. "That'll help. Come sit down and tell me why you don't want to go on the trail ride. Besides the, uh, unpleasantness you're feeling."

She certainly couldn't ignore his gesture, but she

also couldn't ignore her underlying reasons for wanting to beg off on the ride. With a silent sigh, she gingerly placed her sorest area on the pillow, prepared to give him every reason she could think of.

But he settled on the swing beside her, and all reason flew out of her mind.

"The best way to deal with being saddle sore is to get back on again," he explained patiently. "Kind of like the old adage about falling off a horse. That's why there are bathtubs in the cabins." His gaze wandered up the length of her. "They aren't big, but you should fit. A good soak will do wonders."

"But it won't improve my riding skills," she replied, ready to offer her arguments, one by one. "And we both know that I'm about as green as they come."

"Nothing that a private lesson or two won't fix."

She recognized the suggestive, husky tone in his voice. But she also noticed that as soon as he'd said it, he moved away. Not exactly what she would expect, considering that she was certain he had meant to kiss her earlier. If she wasn't careful, they'd be taking up where they left off when they'd been interrupted.

"I'll be honest," she said, ducking her head to stare at the toes of her sneakers. "I can't afford the added expense."

A moment of silence followed. "It's on the house."

So now what should she do? Private lessons wouldn't solve her biggest problem—being near him. But she couldn't come right out and tell him that he did things to her that were completely out of her realm of experience. No man had ever affected her the way he did.

"You really don't want to miss the trail ride," he said, leaning closer. "It's like nothing you've ever experienced. That first ride, out in the open, away from everything, is something that can't be described. Then to wake up in the middle of the night with the stars looking like they're so close you could reach out and grab 'em— Nope, it has to be experienced."

"You sound like a salesman," she said, softening the words with a smile when she looked at him.

He shrugged his broad shoulders. "I suppose I do. But it's the truth." He caught her gaze and held it with eyes burning brightly. "I love this ranch. And I want others to experience the same things I do. If it wasn't this ranch, it would be another one. That's how much it means to me. You'll love it, too."

And she was supposed to say no to this? She couldn't, in spite of knowing she was putting herself—her future and maybe even her heart—in danger. "All right," she said, "I'll take you up on the offer of the private lessons. But only one," she added when she saw victory in his eyes. "I don't want to waste your time."

She moved forward, steeling herself against the pain she knew she would feel when she stood. But Trey was on his feet and offered her his hand. "Slow and easy," he told her, pulling her up gently. "And don't forget to take that long soak in the tub before supper. You'll be glad you did."

But she wondered if she would be glad she'd capitulated to his charm when Sunday came and she started the long drive back to Indiana. Somehow, she doubted it.

* * *

When the phone at Trey's elbow jangled, jarring his already frayed nerves even more, he gave it a scowl, daring it to bring him more bad news. Picking it up, he clamped it to his ear and growled into the receiver. "Triple B Dude Ranch."

"B must stand for bear," the voice on the other end said, accompanied by a deep chuckle.

A smile replaced Trey's frown. "Dev! How the hell are you?"

"Can't complain, baby brother."

At any other time, Trey would have bristled at his brother's choice of words, but he was so damned glad to hear from Dev, he didn't care. Lifting his legs, he propped his boots on the desktop in front of him and leaned back in his chair. "Sure hope you're callin' to say you're headed home."

"In time," Dev replied after a slight hesitation. "In good time. But I've got some news for you."

The muscles in Trey's jaw tightened. *News.* He couldn't take much more. Especially if it had to do with their former neighbor, and he suspected it did.

"Is it about the lawsuit?" he asked.

"No. I'm still waiting to hear from the lawyer. Jimmy Bob's crazy to try this again. The ranch is ours. Every acre of it."

Taking a deep breath, Trey pushed aside thoughts of James Robert Staton, better known as J.R. for the past few years, and slowly let the air out of his lungs. "Then what's the news? Good or bad?"

"Depends on how the Triple B is doing."

Afraid to ask, Trey did anyway. "What's that mean?"

Dev didn't answer immediately, and Trey could hear muffled conversation and noise in the background. Devon Brannigan kept his life a secret. Even Chace, the oldest of the three Brannigan brothers, didn't know where Dev was or what he did.

"Gotta make this quick," Dev said. "I just learned that *Trail's End Magazine* is sending a reporter out to rate the Triple B and do an article. This may be the break you need."

A cold wave of dread seeped down Trey's spine. *Trail's End* was one of the most widely read and respected travel magazines in the country. A good rating could easily make the ranch a complete success. A bad one would mean—

His feet came down on the floor and he straightened in the chair. "When?"

"Far as I know, somebody should be there now."

The chill spread through Trey's bones. Damn. Couldn't this have come some other time? Say, six months down the road? The Triple B needed the good publicity to draw in more guests. But "good" was the operative word. With two of his men out for most of the week and everything going berserk, not to mention his insane preoccupation with Meg Chastain, the ranch could easily fail the test.

"What's the reporter's name?"

"Hell, Trey, I don't know," Dev grumbled. "That's the way *Trail's End* operates. They don't want you to know so you can't butter 'em up for a good rating. But you're smart. You'll figure it out."

Trey closed his eyes and bit off a groan. He had his hands full, as it was. Now this. He might as well chuck it all. The Triple B would be nothing but a failed dream. And his brothers would see that, once again, baby brother couldn't meet the mark.

"Trey? You still there?"

Propping his elbow on the desk, Trey settled his chin in his palm and frowned. "Yeah. Yeah, I'm here. Thanks, Dev. We'll take care of it."

"I know you will. Look, I've gotta go. Tell Chace howdy for me. And good luck. I'll be looking for that article and five-star rating."

"Thanks," Trey said as the click announced the end of the conversation. He'd need all the luck he could get.

Not only had he been fool enough to offer Meg riding lessons—and on the house, when they needed any extra money they could earn—but now he had to deal with finding out who the mysterious reporter was. Damn! Why couldn't he stay away from the woman, like he swore he would?

He pulled a bottle of expensive bourbon from the bookcase behind him and poured a glass, then stood and walked around to the front of the desk. Staring out the window toward the guest cabins, he leaned against the edge of his desk and took a long drink, letting the alcohol burn its way to his gut. It should have cleared his mind. It didn't.

He gazed up at a portrait on the wall, smiled at the familiar face looking down on him and raised his glass in a salute. "Don't worry, Granddaddy. I'll take care of the place. I wasn't named after you and Dad for nothing."

Trey could handle their mystery guest, whoever it was, with no problem. And he wouldn't let any woman get to him and make him forget what was important. The Triple B would always come first.

Chapter Four

Meg watched the campfire flames flicker in the night, occasionally glancing up to catch Trey watching her. He might be spending all his time talking to the other guests, but she had felt his gaze on her throughout the chuckwagon supper and after. He hadn't said a word to her or made a move to join her, and she was glad. Wasn't she?

Of course, she was. She was here to do a job. Nothing more. There wasn't time for a sexy cowboy who turned her insides to the consistency of pudding. She only had four and a half days left to get all the information she could. And not a clue as to how to do it.

Sighing, Meg propped her elbows on her knees and rested her chin in her hands. Maybe she had been wrong thinking she could do this. When she had been offered this opportunity, she'd told her boss that she had some ranching experience when she was a child. Okay, so she'd exaggerated. But old reruns of *Bonanza* and *The Big Valley* counted for something. Geraldine had not only been desperate, but she had been impressed and said Meg could look at it as getting back to her roots.

"Back to my roots," she muttered, "I'll give her—"

"I brought somebody to meet you."

Meg looked up to see Trey standing to her right with a petite blond woman at his side. Was it possible Trey was engaged? Or even…married? No, he couldn't be. He wouldn't have almost kissed her earlier. Right? She certainly hoped not. Then again, maybe he was nothing more than a cowboy Casanova.

The woman held out her hand. "Howdy. I'm Ellie. Chace's wife."

Meg shook her hand and realized that if Ellie was Chace's wife… "You're the riding instructor! And Chace is the one with the horses."

Ellie nodded. "That's him. I hope you've been enjoying yourself."

"Oh, I have. It's so peaceful here and yet there's so much to keep me busy." Since she hadn't done much besides participate in one riding lesson, Meg couldn't say what she specifically liked. "Will you be teaching the riding class tomorrow?"

Trey steered Ellie to the empty seat next to Meg. "Feeling better?" he asked Meg.

She wasn't sure how to answer, considering how her body still ached from the first ride. Even a long soak hadn't put an end to her discomfort. But she had a feeling that the lesson would be different with Ellie teaching it. "I'll see if I'm up to it in the morning," she said, with a wry smile.

Ellie laughed. "Yeah, it can be a sore point for someone who hasn't ridden. But to answer your question, yes, I'll be teaching the class in the morning. It's usually my job, but our secretary has been gone the past two days, so I needed to fill in for her."

"So that's why Trey was teaching it this morning," Meg said, beginning to understand.

Ellie shot Trey a wicked grin before turning back to Meg. "Right. And it's not his favorite activity, either."

"Sherry should be back in the office tomorrow," Trey added, "so everything will be back to normal."

"Have you been riding long?" Meg asked Ellie.

"Since I was a kid. How about you?"

"Today was my first time."

"It won't take long to get the hang of it," Ellie told her with a smile and another glance at Trey.

"Ellie raced barrels at National Finals before she gave it up for married life," Trey said with a chuckle.

Meg was impressed. "Then you obviously know how to ride."

"You could say that," Ellie said, smiling. "But in spite of what Trey says and the fact that Chace and I met on the circuit, I didn't give up rodeoing for married life. I raced barrels for more years than I like to think. It was time to retire."

Meg couldn't imagine anyone retiring so young. She guessed Ellie was about her age, but it would be a long, long time before her own retirement.

"You'll have to excuse us, Meg," Trey said, offering

a hand to Ellie and helping her to her feet, "but we have some business to take care of."

Ellie groaned. "Back to work. It was nice meeting you, Meg. I'm looking forward to helping you with your riding tomorrow."

"Thanks. I'm looking forward to it, too." Meg watched them as they walked away to join several of the other ranch employees, and then all of them headed for the ranch house. She wished she could find out what was going on, but other than following them and lurking outside a window, there wasn't much she could do. With luck, she might learn something later. She needed to talk to the owner, Buford Brannigan, but she had yet to find him. As soon as the opportunity presented itself, she'd find a way to ask someone. Until then, she would have to wait.

"Any idea who it might be?" Trey asked the others when he had finished telling them about Dev's call.

Pete scratched his neck and cleared his throat. "There's one fella."

Trey was happy to hear they might have a clue. "Who?"

"Name's Emery. Richard, I think. The fella I was talkin' to at the campfire."

Scanning the list of guests on the desk in front of him, Trey found the name. "He's from Illinois. Or at least, that's what this says. You might check his license plate. *Trail's End* is published in Chicago. Could be a coincidence. What makes you think he might be the one?"

Pete chuckled and shook his head. "You gotta meet him for yourself."

"Real greenhorn, huh? Okay, I'll take care of—" He glanced at the list again and stabbed the name on the paper with a finger, a slow smile creeping over his face. "Mr. Emery. If he's the one, we'll show him what dude ranching is all about and get that five-star rating for the Triple B. Thanks, Pete."

Pete tugged his hat down and stood. "Glad to help."

"Tell the rest of the boys to keep their eyes and ears open," Trey added. "Same goes for the rest of you," he told the others as they started to leave. "This is top priority."

When everyone had gone except Chace and Ellie, Trey leaned back in his chair. "Looks like we've got a good chance to do the Triple B proud and get the word out."

Chace moved to take the chair Pete had vacated next to his wife. "I don't know if this is such a good idea."

Ellie nodded in agreement. "Are you sure this Richard Emery is the reporter from *Trail's End?* I mean, it could be anybody, right?"

"I'm pretty sure it is." Trey leaned forward and clasped his hands on the desk. "No concrete evidence, of course, but there's nobody else who comes close. And now that I think of it, I was giving him riding lessons this morning. The man uses twenty-dollar words, and he's real eager to learn."

Ellie looked at Chace and then shrugged. "That sounds reasonable. But shouldn't you keep an eye on the rest, just in case you're wrong?"

Pushing away from the desk, Trey stood and picked up his hat. "I'm a fair judge of people. If I weren't, I wouldn't be in this business." But he wasn't so sure of himself, considering that he didn't have Meg figured out yet. But he would.

"There's nothing wrong with the Triple B," Chace said, frowning. "The guests are happy, aren't they?"

"Sure they are," Trey answered, while Ellie nodded in agreement. "I just want to make sure we give this Emery guy the right impression."

"You do a good job handling the guests, baby brother," Chace continued. "But you might want to take it easy. If the Triple B's going to get a good rating, let it be an honest one. Not because you did something for one particular guest you wanted to impress."

"I'd agree, but—"

"Good," Chace said, standing and helping his wife to her feet. "Did Dev say anything about J.R.?"

With a humorless laugh, Trey shook his head. "Nope. He's waiting to hear from the lawyer."

Chace nodded as he and Ellie turned to leave. "It's better that Dev's handling this. I don't know how or why, but he seems to know what he's doing."

"He must have some connections somewhere, but I doubt we'll ever know for sure," Trey agreed.

As Chace and Ellie opened the door and stepped out of the room, Trey thought of pointing out how badly the Triple B needed a good rating from Emery and *Trail's End.* But he thought better of it. He'd do all the buttering up that was necessary. In fact, now was a good time to start.

Tired and saddle sore, Meg decided to call it a night. The evening hadn't been a total waste, she thought as she started back for her cabin. She'd met Ellie and learned a little personal history about her. The romantic meeting of Ellie and her husband would be something—

"You're lost in thought."

Meg jumped at the sound of the rich baritone, the voice sending shivers of heat through her. "I-I was just thinking," she replied. Trey was so close, she nearly forgot to breathe. "Thank you for introducing me to Ellie. It was nice of her to go out of her way to talk to me."

Trey matched his steps to hers. "Aw, Meg. We're not going out of our way. That's just the way we are. Friendly."

She nearly choked. Trey had gone beyond the point of friendly, and she hadn't bothered to stop him, making her the one at fault.

When they reached her cabin door, she turned to regard him with a smile. "Are all the cowboys in Texas as friendly as you are?"

She knew she was in trouble when he tipped her chin up with one finger and looked down at her. "I sure hope not."

They stood that way for what seemed like an eternity. Meg swore he had to hear her heart pounding in her chest and spoke to cover the sound of it. "Wh-why not?" she managed to ask, although her voice had pretty much deserted her.

His breath whispered across her face. Meg's bones turned to mush, and she had to lean against the door to keep from falling in a puddle. Unable to think straight, all she could do was make sure she was still breathing.

Still tipping her head back, he scooted her glasses

back up the bridge of her nose with his free hand.
"Maybe I should call you Magoo."

"Magoo?"

His nod was so slight, she barely caught it. "Would
you like that?" he asked, his whisper now husky, skipping like a stone.over the ripples inside her.

"M-Meg is just fine."

"Whatever you say, Meg."

The way he said it sent shivers through her, making
her tremble.

"Cold, Meg?"

Cold? How could she be cold with him so near?
Speechless, she shook her head. It surprised her that her
glasses hadn't fogged over with all the heat generating
between them. She felt like she was on fire from the inside out. But she certainly wouldn't tell him that.

His toe-curling grin broke out. "Warm?"

She closed her eyes, swallowed, and nodded.

When he released her and took a step back, she shiv-
ered from the absence of his warmth. Until a chuckle
rumbled up from his chest. "Yeah, me, too."

Without another word, he bounded down the two
steps of the tiny porch and disappeared into the night.

She let out a long-held breath. How would she ever
keep her mind on the review if that cowboy kept doing
things to her she couldn't fight?

"Where have you been?" Trey asked Meg late the
next morning. "You missed the riding lesson."

She closed the door of her car and looked up, surprise
widening her eyes. "I talked to Ellie before I left. I'm

sorry Sherry didn't show up for work again. Did you have to teach the lesson?"

"Don't worry about it. Ellie took over," he said, more concerned with where Meg had gone than his missing secretary. He knew he was sounding like a spoiled kid, but he didn't care. He'd been worried. He hadn't seen hide nor hair of Meg since the night before. "Ellie didn't mention that you were going to be gone."

"Maybe she forgot," she answered, turning in the direction of her cabin. "I asked her for directions into San Antonio, and she gave me the name of the best store where I could get a pair of boots. See?" Grinning, she held up a sack which obviously contained a large box. "I thought it might be better to have them before I climbed on a horse again."

"I could've gone with you and showed you around San Antone."

"I didn't want to bother you."

Before he could say that it wouldn't have been a bother at all, he stopped. What was wrong with him? He'd never cared where his little darlin's were when they weren't with him. And he shouldn't care what Meg did with her time. After all, she was a guest. So maybe he just wanted to make sure that she was having a good time, the same as he did with all the other guests.

"Now that you've bought boots, this would be a good time for that private lesson," he said instead.

She slid him a look. "Are you sure? I mean, if you're busy—"

"I'm sure. The sooner we start, the sooner you'll be riding as good as Ellie."

Meg's laughter caught him off guard, and he almost stumbled. Except for her strange taste in clothes, wasn't there anything he could find about her that he didn't enjoy?

"I'll be happy just to be able to mount and keep control of a horse," she said, more seriously.

He was sure that could be done and hoped for even more. "You get changed and I'll get the horses ready," he told her. "I'll meet you at the corral."

It didn't take him long to saddle both Temptation and Moonlight. After he had finished, he stood at the corral fence, his arms folded on the top rail, one boot propped on the bottom one, and waited for Meg.

Meg. The name had tasted like sweet honey last night when he'd said it. He'd nearly lost it when she'd trembled at his touch. Most women he knew would have cozied right up to him. But not Meg. And that pleased him. She might not dress like a woman filled with burning passion, but he'd bet she'd respond to lovemaking like a house on fire. Too bad he wouldn't be the man to strike the match.

"Don't you have nothin' to do, boss?"

Trey cocked his head to see Pete settle next to him. "Got plenty to do. Just taking a little break."

"Thought you were going to keep an eye on that Emery fella."

"What do you think I'm doing?"

Pete chuckled. "Not much of anything, since he ain't even around here."

Turning, Trey scowled at their head wrangler. "What makes you think so?"

This time, Pete roared with laughter. Seeing that he'd

spooked some of the horses, he ducked his head. "You've been spending a lot of time with that Chastain woman. She caught your eye, huh?"

Trey didn't know whether to admit to the attraction or hotly deny it. If he admitted he found Meg sexier than all of his little darlin's put together, he'd never live it down. On the other hand, if he denied it, Pete would keep needling him. Having spent most of his adult life with the cowboy, Trey knew how he thought.

A shrug was all he could manage.

"Thought so," Pete said, choking on quiet laughter.

Trey groaned and pressed his forehead to his arms. He wasn't up for this. Shoving away from the fence, he faced Pete. Giving him a friendly slap on the shoulder, Trey grinned. "Doesn't much matter what you think."

"Well, you've always been good with women."

Trey shot him a grin. "That's it, Pete." But if he was so good with women, why hadn't he gone through with that kiss he wanted to give her last night? Damn, the woman was getting to him. Any other time, he'd have had his hands full of warm, willing female. With Meg, he wanted to pull her close, but it just didn't feel the same way. Not the same way at all.

He wanted to kiss her, to feel his lips pressed to hers, to slip his tongue between those lips and taste her sweet mouth the way it begged to be tasted. Hell, he was dying to kiss her. So why hadn't he? He'd lain awake most of the night trying to figure it out. At the rate he was going, with this slow and steady plodding, it'd be Christmas before he worked his way to anything remotely intimate. And Meg would be long gone by then.

Then again, so would his peace of mind, because she was chipping away at it, bit by bit.

"Looks like the object of your affection is here."

Trey turned around to see Meg walking toward him. To his disappointment, she was wearing a seriously oversize T-shirt that looked as if she'd stolen it from a bouncer in the toughest bar in Texas. "You just keep Emery happy," he told Pete. "I'll take care of Miss Chastain."

"Yeah, I'll bet you will," Pete muttered and laughed as he walked away.

"Nervous?" Trey asked Meg when she reached him.

"Not as much as I was yesterday."

"Then let's get to it," he said, eager to get the lesson started. If he couldn't do the things he wanted to do with her, then he'd make sure that by the time supper rolled around, she was a pretty fair horsewoman. "Think you can mount without any help?"

Meg's teeth sank into her full bottom lip, and Trey nearly lost control. Oh, he was going to pay for this. In triplicate.

As he watched her, unable to look at anything else, she took a deep breath and squared her shoulders. "I can sure try."

It took her two tries, but on the second, she gracefully mounted her horse. Her look of sheer pleasure at her success had Trey grinning. He walked to his own horse and swung up into the saddle. "Let me see you walk him around."

With her face set in sheer concentration, Meg nudged Moonlight into a walk. In only a few minutes, she was grinning. "You know, this is fun," she told him over her shoulder.

He returned the grin. He had been right. She would be riding circles around the other guests before the day was out. "Now try putting him into a trot," he called to her. "Watch me, and then do the same thing."

She watched carefully and then imitated his actions, urging her horse into a fairly smooth trot. "It's kind of bumpy," she said, but she didn't look like it bothered her much.

After a couple of turns around the corral he showed her how to slow back down to a walk. "You'll like loping a lot better," he assured her. "But you've probably heard it called cantering. Whatever, let's give it a try and see how you do."

Once again, he demonstrated and, like before, Meg mastered it quickly. "I can't imagine what it's like to run with him," she said when she slowed and pulled up beside him, breathless from her ride.

"He's got a smooth gallop," he told her, "but there isn't room here in the corral for you to try it. When we're out in the open on the trail ride, you can let him loose."

"I'm really looking forward to the trail ride now." Giving him a sheepish grin, she ducked her head. "I guess I was pretty much afraid of horses before. Not to mention saddle sore."

Trey nodded. "And you'll be sore again tonight if you don't take a good long soak before supper." He swung down from off horse and walked over to her. "But first, we need to get these saddles off and give both these horses a good brushing. Ellie will be madder than a wet hen if we leave her with two sweaty horses."

Meg nodded, her face serious. He could tell that she wasn't as sure about dismounting as she now was about riding. "Need some help?" he asked.

Her head whipped around and she stared at him. Her smile was quick but forced. "I think I can do it by myself this time."

He couldn't deny that he was a little disappointed. But he was glad he hadn't insisted when she swung off the horse like a pro.

"Hey, that's pretty good!" Ellie called to them from the fence. "I knew Trey would be a good teacher if he put his mind to it."

"We were just finishing up," Trey told her, as he helped Meg take her horse to the barn.

"I'll help," Ellie said as she climbed over the fence. "If you don't mind," she whispered to him with a wicked grin when she'd caught up with him.

He shot her a warning glare. "Why don't you take Temptation on in and get started," he said, handing her the reins. "Before I forget, I'll run up to the house and get that bottle of liniment." He let his gaze wander up the back of Meg. "She may be feelin' fine now, but…" He grinned at Meg when she turned around to look at him. "We'll get you fixed up," he told her with a wink.

As he walked to the house, he had to admit that he had enjoyed instructing Meg. In spite of her initial fear of horses, she was a natural. He shouldn't have doubted it. Hadn't he been fascinated with the way she moved when she wasn't on a horse? And just where would that fascination end, he wondered.

"The Triple B is doing okay, isn't it?" Meg asked, brushing the horse as Ellie had taught her. "I mean, everything looks great and everybody seems to be having a great time."

"It's doing okay," Ellie replied, hidden behind the horse she was grooming. "And if we get in more groups like this one, it'll be even better. A few good words in *Trail's End* could give us a really big break."

Meg caught her breath and held it. What should she say? It couldn't be anything that might arouse Ellie's suspicions, but she had to say something.

"Trail's End?" she finally managed.

"Yeah, it's a travel magazine for the western crowd." Ellie peeked at her around the horse's head. "Or the western wannabes," she added with a wink. "Lots of dude ranches, Native American places, historic sites. Most in the western states, but some back east, too."

Setting her face in an interested but innocent mask, Meg nodded. "So why not put an ad in this magazine?"

"We have," Ellie said, going back to her grooming. "But Dev called and said they've sent a reporter to check out the place for a rating and an article. If it's good enough, people will start visiting the place in herds."

Meg had only one question. "Who's the reporter?"

"Trey's pretty sure it's Richard Emery. I have to say I agree with him. The man is just full of questions."

Relief flooded Meg. She'd played her role well. No one was the wiser as to her true purpose for being at the

Triple B. Thank heaven she hadn't asked too many questions and given herself away. And bless Mr. Richard Emery for being an inquisitive person.

Still, there was one person whose place in all this she hadn't quite figured out. "What about—"

"Hey, Ellie! You in here?"

Stepping around the horse, Ellie answered. "Yeah, what do you need?"

Meg looked down to the other end of the barn to see one of the ranch hands.

"Trey needs you up at the house," he called, jerking a thumb in the direction of the main house.

Ellie shrugged and smiled at Meg before shouting back. "Be right there." She handed Meg the curry comb. "Think you can finish this one for me?"

"I'll try," Meg assured her.

Meg had no problem grooming the horse. She'd quickly learned that as long as she didn't show her fear or nervousness, she and the animal got along well.

Finished with one side, she moved to the other. Each stroke brought her another thin slice of peace. Why was it, she wondered, that the basic tasks in life calmed her nerves? She loved her job, but even at the best of times, it was stressful. She'd needed a vacation. Her climb from simple receptionist to the chance to become a full-fledged staff writer had taken her six years. It hadn't been easy. Each and every step had taken a piece of her. But she hoped it had been more than well worth the effort.

She leaned around to look at Moonlight. "Has it been worth it?"

"Only if you're happy."

Meg squealed, causing the horse to sidestep nervously. Before she knew what was happening, she was pulled into a pair of strong arms and hugged tight against a broad, equally strong chest.

"Damn. I didn't know I'd scare you."

Looking up into a pair of familiar blue eyes, Meg took a deep breath and let it out. "Well, you did. You can let me go now. I'm fine."

"Yeah, you sure are," Trey said, his voice rough and his breathing uneven. "But I can't figure out why."

Meg felt like the breath she'd taken had been her last. With her knees turning to the consistency of jelly, she could barely stand. He'd nearly kissed her twice. Would he try a third? And did she want him to?

When he reached up to touch her hair, Meg came to life. Shoving at his rock hard chest, she pulled away.

"What'd I do?" he asked, his expression innocent.

"Nothing."

Tugging at the hem of her shirt, she tried to calm her fears. She'd kissed enough men to know she'd never failed to be disappointed. She'd even worried she might be unable to feel anything for any man. She'd barred the thought from her mind, successfully getting on with her life without worrying about it. Until now. Until she'd arrived at the Triple B and met a cowboy with a drop-dead gorgeous smile and hips that swiveled like Elvis's.

"Meg."

Tiny lightening bolts skittered along her nerves.

Taking a step closer, Trey lifted his hand and removed her glasses. "I won't hurt you."

Unable to utter a sound, she shook her head.

"Does that mean you believe me?" he asked with a lopsided grin. "Or that you think I'm lying?"

Meg didn't know what she meant. All she knew was that one of them would get hurt if she allowed this to go another step further. Past relationships had taught her that the men she had been involved with had been disappointed, though not nearly as disappointed as she had always been. Both in them and in herself. She didn't want that to happen this time. She couldn't risk losing the feelings Trey made her feel whenever he was around. She'd rather take those home with her, never knowing more, than be left with nothing except the hollowness she had become accustomed to in the past.

"I'm not going to throw you down in the hay and take liberties with you," he assured her. "I just want…"

She held her breath, waiting for him to finish. His gaze held hers as sure as a magnet to steel.

"Just a kiss, Meg. Nothing more. I swear."

Dare she risk it? She couldn't answer. Closing her eyes, she gathered her courage. But before she was ready, she felt his callused hands framing her face. She didn't have to see him to know what was happening. Days passed as she stood waiting for his lips to touch hers. Weeks. Years. When they finally did, she was prepared for the usual disappointment.

Not this time. This time, instead of a nothingness seeping into her soul, a tidal wave of heat swept through her. He feathered kisses across her lips, teasing her and making her ache for more. When she thought she couldn't stand it any longer, was ready to plead with him, she felt his firm mouth cover hers. Weak with surrender, she leaned into him, her breasts pressing against his chest.

His hands moved from her face, down her shoulders to skim along her arms to her wrists. And his teasing didn't stop. When the tip of his tongue caressed the sensitive bow of her lips, she gasped, allowing his entry. So different than the forceful entry of others' kisses, he proceeded with tender caution. She pressed against him, touching him with every inch of her body that she could. Lifting her wrists, he brought her arms to circle his neck, bringing the two of them even closer together. She threaded her fingers in the hair that brushed his nape, and his groan vibrated through her, heating her to her soul. His arms held her, pulling her closer, molding her body to his. Stroking her mouth with his tongue, he sent rivers of desire flowing through her. Tentatively, her tongue met his, and tremors of need shook her.

She didn't know how long they stayed locked together. Time lost all meaning for her. He gentled the kiss, nipping at her lips as her breathing grew more ragged. When he moved to press kisses along her neck, she knew she'd discovered the meaning of passion.

"We shouldn't be doing this," she whispered as reality began to slowly return.

"I know," he replied, his breathing as halted and heavy as hers.

"Someone could—"

She didn't finish as he claimed her mouth again, punishing her with a second kiss. His hands moved along her back, smoothing and caressing, pulling her even closer until the fire between them nearly scorched her with the need for more.

"Damn, Meg," he said when he finally, gently, released her.

She looked into his eyes, darkened to navy with a passion she knew rivaled her own. "Trey, we can't…I can't…"

"Shhh," he said before kissing her again, softly, with a gentleness that made her want to weep. "All I wanted was a kiss. That's all. And now—" His smile was almost melancholy. "And now I have to let you go, because—"

"It can't go any further," she finished for him.

His silence frightened her, and when he finally spoke, she wished he hadn't. "I never should have started it."

She couldn't bear to look at him and see the regret in his eyes. "I wanted you to."

He tipped her head to force her to join her gaze with his. "You did?"

Air whooshed out of her as disappointment filled its place. Once again, she'd failed to respond the way most women did. Trey couldn't guess at what he'd made her feel. "I think I should go shower and change," she said without answering his question. She escaped his embrace and gave a nervous yank to the hem of her shirt.

She turned to leave, but Trey took her hand, bringing her to a stop. His expression shouted regret as his gaze searched her face. "I'm sorry, Meg. I didn't mean to—"

"Don't worry about it." She pulled her hand from his and waved it in the air, dismissing anything more he might say. She couldn't bear to have him apologize when it wasn't his fault. It was hers. She'd always thought she must be lacking something. Just like her mother, who never could keep a man around long enough to build a relationship. If her father had loved them enough, he wouldn't have left them when she was two. She'd always wondered how long her stepfather would have stayed if her mother hadn't died. He certainly hadn't stayed long to take care of a motherless Meg.

Hardening her heart, she tossed Trey a bright smile she hoped looked genuine, and hurried from the barn. She'd make sure nothing like this ever happened again.

Chapter Five

Staring at the campfire flames, Trey wondered what the hell he had done. Ever since the kiss he'd shared with Meg in the barn, she'd done her best to avoid him. At that moment, she was sitting with the Hendersons, looking like she didn't have a care in the world. As if that kiss meant nothing to her. Dammit, it meant something to him. He hadn't planned for or even expected it to, but it did. He had thought she felt the same way. As soon as he'd touched his lips to hers, it was as if he'd ignited something in her. It had only taken seconds for him to feel the same flames engulfing him. Not like any other kiss he ever remembered.

But when it had ended, when she'd pulled away from him after admitting she'd wanted it, something happened. Something changed. She'd left him with a smile that was as fake as a two dollar bill. And he hadn't expected that from Meg.

He was crazy to want more, but he did. He was crazy to even consider getting involved with someone who would be leaving in a few days. But that didn't usually bother him. He wasn't a man who wanted any sort of commitment. He never planned to settle down with one woman. Nope, not him. He liked variety in his life, not a steady diet of the same. At least where women were concerned.

"Go ahead, ignore me," he muttered under his breath.

"Talking to yourself, little brother?"

Trey's answer was a grunt. Chace was the last person he wanted to talk to right now. Chace wouldn't understand.

"She giving you trouble?"

"Women don't give me trouble," Trey replied. They never had before, anyway, and he wasn't about to let them start now. Glancing at his brother, he grinned, but it was painful. "They've always told me *I* was trouble."

Chace returned the smile. "So I've heard," he said with a chuckle.

But Trey had to admit, Meg was beginning to get to him. Had been since before the kiss. And now...

Chace leaned closer. "You know, the dance is tomorrow night. Maybe you can make something happen."

"Damn, Chace, who said I wanted something to happen?" Trey snapped. "And who said something hasn't already?"

"Uh-oh. Did you get shut down, little brother?"

"Hell, no," Trey lied.

Chace nudged him with his shoulder. "Then why aren't you over there talking to her?"

Talk? The last thing he wanted to do with Meg was

talk. He didn't need words to find out if he'd imagined her response to his kiss. Hell, he hadn't imagined it.

"I'll show you how a man who knows how to handle women does it." He pushed his way through the row of guests seated in front of him and marched across the circle, skirting the campfire, to stand in front of Meg. "Howdy, folks," he told the others with his most charming smile. Grabbing Meg's hand, he pulled her to her feet. "I need to borrow Miss Chastain for a minute."

As he hauled her away from the other guests, she tried to pull away. "Let go, Trey."

"Nope." He held her hand even tighter. He didn't stop, either, until he had her far enough away from the campfire that nobody would bother them. Only then did he let go, but only to wrap her in his arms. "I need to satisfy a little curiosity."

Heedless of her hands pushing at his chest and the sounds of her protests, he dipped his head to capture her lips.

It only took a second for her to respond to his kiss, canceling her resistance and replacing it with a passion that made his head spin. She wove her hands around his neck, and he pulled her even closer, needing to feel her body's slightest movement. But all he felt was heat, burning him with an intensity he'd never experienced. And he couldn't stop. Like a drug, the taste of her, the feel of her, was all he craved.

Forcing himself to end the kiss, he released her and took a deep breath to steady himself. "Don't say you didn't feel anything this time," he said as he walked away.

"Trey!"

He ignored her and kept walking until he was sure he'd disappeared from her view. Just like she'd walked away from him that afternoon. She might be getting to him, but he wasn't addicted yet. And he sure as hell didn't intend to be.

"She said what?" Trey demanded.

Meg looked up from her plate of fluffy scrambled eggs and saw Trey talking to Ellie.

"She got married last night, Trey," Ellie said, the frustration in her voice evident. "She and Dave eloped to Louisiana and she called from there."

From her vantage point, Meg could see the disgust and anger on Trey's face. Her heart sank. Obviously some woman's marriage had him upset. Very upset. And here she'd been obsessing about the kisses they'd shared. Even though she'd tossed and turned all night, trying to force the memory of them from her mind, her body still hummed. Knowing she shouldn't be eavesdropping, she did anyway, pretending to be interested in her breakfast, but straining to hear every word she could.

"Well that's just dandy," Trey bit out. "And what are we supposed to do in the meantime? We're already short-handed."

Meg couldn't make out what Ellie said to him, but his answer was loud and clear. "I can't. Pete needs help getting things ready for the trail ride on Saturday. I'm not some errand-boy nobody around here."

"And I have a riding class to teach in fifteen minutes," Ellie replied, her voice rising. "Chace is dealing with the herd. Pete's busy with the trail ride. Do you have any suggestions?"

"One," Trey shouted. "I'm going to wring Sherry's neck the next time she so much as shows her face around here."

Ellie shook her head. "She won't be back. She pretty much quit. So we're without a secretary until we can hire someone else, or at least find a temp to fill in for a while. Until then, somebody has to answer the phones and check on reservations and everything else."

Meg didn't even realize she'd gotten to her feet until she heard herself speak. "I can fill in for Sherry."

Ellie and Trey swung around to stare at her, and Ellie stepped forward. "That's very sweet of you, but—"

"I'd like to do something." Meg looked from Ellie to Trey, who was frowning at her and shaking his head.

"This is your vacation, Meg." Ellie smiled and glanced at Trey. "I can't take advantage of your generosity, but thank you for offering." She turned back to Trey. "We'll make up a schedule. Everyone can take a turn."

"And we'll get nothing done," Trey said, his frown deepening. "Chace will be the first to tell you. This is a working dude ranch. *Working*. Got it?"

Meg approached him and laid her hand on his arm. "I've spent years doing office work. Please, let me help."

Pulling away from her, Trey shook his head. "Forget it. We'll work something out."

Meg wasn't going to take no for an answer. She turned to Ellie. "It'll only take a few minutes for you to show me what to do, and then you can concentrate on the riding lessons."

"I don't know…"

Trey swore under his breath. "I'll show you," he said, taking Meg by the arm. Steering her toward the main house, his voice sounded odd. "Just answer the phone if it rings. Don't do anything else."

"Ellie," Meg called over her shoulder, "when you're done with the lesson, come show me what else you want me to do."

"I'll be the one telling you," Trey said.

She looked up to see his dark brows drawn together in a scowl and his lips in a tight line. "I don't know what you're so mad about, but you can let go of me," she insisted, prying his fingers from her arm.

Opening the heavy oak door, he let her pass and led her down the stone-floored hallway. When they came to the office at the back of the house, he opened the door and waved her into the room. She sailed past him and crossed her arms beneath her breasts, waiting for him to follow. "I only want to help."

"Thanks," he replied, but it was said grudgingly. Moving to stand behind the desk, he straightened a pile of papers which were spread out over the top. "Just answer the phone and tell whoever calls that someone will get back to them."

"You could let the answering machine do that for you," she pointed out.

"Some people don't like those contraptions." Without a glance at her, he strode to the door. "When Ellie's done with the lessons, you're free. We'll handle it from there."

Meg nodded, feeling as if he were dismissing her and

not knowing what she'd done to deserve this treatment. When he'd gone without another word, she circled the desk and sank onto the worn leather chair, looking around.

It was a man's office. A busy man's office. Piles of papers and file folders littered the desk. A half-wall of bookshelves behind the desk held books on ranching and animal husbandry, with a computer tucked beneath. A map of the area stretched along the wall beside the door, but when Meg stood and walked over to take a look at it, she discovered that it wasn't a map of the Banderas, but of the Triple B Ranch.

Impressed with the size of the spread, although she knew the acreage to be in the six digits, Meg studied it. Balancing on the arm of a well-padded but worn leather wingback chair, she ran her finger over marks of twisting trails and wondered how much of the ranch she'd be seeing on the trail ride.

When the phone rang, she crossed to the desk and answered it. "Triple B Dude Ranch. This is Meg. May I help you?"

"This is Wayne Garrison at Garrison Feed Store over here in Stakeout," the man on the other end of the line said. "Where's Sherry?"

"I'm filling in for her today, sir," Meg replied. She didn't feel it was her place to tell him that Sherry wouldn't be back.

"Dang, girl. You've got some nice manners."

Swallowing her laughter, Meg managed to thank him. "Is there a special reason for your call, Mr. Garrison?"

"Call me Wayne. Everybody does. I was supposed to

call when we got in the shipment Trey ordered, so that's what I'm doin'."

Meg jotted the message on a pad of paper and promised him she'd make sure it got to the right person. Replacing the receiver, she looked up at the sound of the door opening to see Trey amble into the room. He eyed the top of desk in front of her and let out his breath. "How's it going?"

"Fine." Meg relayed the phone message.

Trey nodded as he approached the desk. Meg watched him dig through one stack of papers after another. When she couldn't stand it any longer, she pulled a stack toward her. "If you'll tell me what you're looking for—"

Wrapping his long, tanned fingers around her wrist, he drew her hand away. "I'll find it."

Meg huffed out an exasperated breath and crossed her arms on her chest to keep from shoving him out of the way. "You know, if things were filed in the file cabinet, you wouldn't have to dig around to find them."

"Aha!" He held up a sheet of paper that looked like an invoice, and then shot her a triumphant smile. "I don't have any trouble finding things."

Meg looked heavenward, shook her head and closed her eyes. "You just spent two minutes for what should have taken five seconds."

His eyes narrowed as he looked at her. "What do you know about it?"

Uncrossing her arms, Meg placed her hands on the desk and leaned toward him. "I've worked in offices since I was sixteen. I'd say that's long enough to know what works and what doesn't." She straightened and swept her hand through the air. "Is it always like this? Or is it only since Sherry's been gone?"

Trey's head dipped, his hat shadowing his face. "Always is, I guess," he mumbled.

"What did Sherry do around here?" When Trey shrugged, she threw her hands in the air. "You mean you paid her to do nothing except answer the phone?"

"I don't know," he replied. "Seems like she was never real busy. She was always doing her nails or something when I came in. But she did her job, as far as I know."

Scooping up a stack of file folders, Meg marched to the four-drawer file cabinet. "I'll just start with these."

As she pulled the top drawer open, he stepped up behind her and reached around for the papers in her hand. "I don't want you doin' this."

Meg glanced over her shoulder to see him looking at her. His blue eyes were unreadable. He was so close to her, the heat of his body warmed her. All she needed to do was lean back to bring herself in contact with him. She wanted to—oh, she wanted to—but she didn't.

"Why not?" she asked, her voice a husky whisper.

His free hand snaked around her waist and he leaned forward. "Aw, hell, Meg," he said as he dipped his head towards her.

The sound of the door opening again was followed by Ellie's voice. "Oh, Meg, I'm so sorry, I'm—"

Meg froze, not knowing what to do.

Trey shoved the file drawer back in with one hand, catching a file, while he let go of Meg with the other and pulled the next drawer open. "Just showin' Meg where these papers go."

"I…thought I'd try and straighten up a little," Meg offered with a shaky voice. Freed, she squeezed out of the space between Trey and the drawer. Moving to the desk, she grabbed another pile of papers. She dared a glance at Ellie, who stood in the doorway, one eyebrow raised and a know-it-all smile on her face.

"Uh-huh," Ellie said, her smile as wide as the Cheshire cat's.

Meg felt her face heat up with embarrassment, and ducked her head to hide it. "I'll just get these sorted."

When the file drawer slammed shut, both women stared at Trey. Making his way to the door, he looked like a little boy who had just been caught with his hand in the cookie jar. "Sorry. I'll just…" He looked from Meg to Ellie and quickened his steps. "I'll get back to work." Skirting around Ellie, who still stood in the doorway, he lit out like someone was after him with a shotgun.

"Well," Ellie said, covering what Meg suspected was a laugh with a cough. "Let me give you a hand with that."

Meg waved her away and picked up a brochure like the one Geraldine had given her for this assignment. "I'll get this filing system straightened out and everything put away. Trey only wants me to take messages, but if you show me how, maybe I can book some reservations if anyone calls about one."

"Everything's in the brochure," Ellie said with a nod at the paper in Meg's hand, the awkwardness of the situation obviously past her. "And somewhere on the desk, or maybe in the drawer, there should be a reservation book where you can put the information. There's no reason why you can't do it. I don't know what's eating Trey. Maybe it makes him nervous having somebody who can actually do things in this office. Sherry wasn't worth much, but she was all we could get."

Meg moved to the filing cabinet to rescue the crumpled file. "I would think anyone would be happy to work here."

"Too far out of town for most people," Ellie said as she picked up a pile of papers and began sorting them into piles. "And we can't pay a lot yet. But maybe it'll get better."

"If we work together, maybe we can make heads or tails of this mess," Meg answered, taking a seat behind the desk.

"I'll sort the papers and folders, while you familiarize yourself with the file cabinet."

Meg agreed it was the perfect solution to tidying the office, and twenty minutes later, the two of them had the desk neat.

"Thanks for all your help, Meg. It looks great, but I need to get back out there," Ellie said with a wave as Meg answered another call. "See you later."

On the phone, Meg answered questions about what the Triple B had to offer, pleased that she could give a glowing and honest reply. She'd heard enough talk between the other guests to know that every one of them was pleased with what the ranch had to offer. Richard Emery, especially, had high praise, and the thought brought a smile to Meg's lips. It wouldn't be difficult at all to write a positive review. Everything she'd seen so far had been excellent in the way of activities, service and all-around friendliness and enjoyment.

Between taking calls and making reservations, she managed to make a list of all the files in the cabinet. It wouldn't take her long to come up with a system the Triple B would find a vast improvement and easy to use.

The next time the door opened, she glanced up from her work to find Trey looking around the room, his eyes wide.

"Like it?" she asked.

He turned his gaze to her and frowned. "What did you do with everything?" he demanded.

"It's filed away. Ellie showed me where everything goes."

Stuffing his hands in his pockets, he looked away. "You can go now. I'll take over."

Meg wanted to ask him what it was that she'd done to earn his disapproval, but it was clear he wasn't in the mood to talk. And by the look on his face, he wasn't in the mood to be in her company either. Still, considering their last unbusinesslike encounter the night before, she couldn't let him off.

Keeping her eyes on the desktop, she took a deep breath and jumped in. "What's bothering you, Trey? Is there something in these papers I shouldn't see? Some deep, dark secret about the Triple B?"

"Of course not," he snapped.

She stood and walked around the desk to stand in front of him. "Then what is it? It's clear that you don't want me helping. Why not just tell me why?"

A muscle in his jaw jumped as he stood silently before her. "You're supposed to be on your vacation," he said when he finally spoke, his voice low and his eyes averted. "You didn't pay good money to come here to work."

"But I don't mind," she replied. Wanting to reach out and touch him, she didn't, knowing he'd only draw away from her.

"Then you aren't enjoying yourself."

"But I am!" she insisted. "It isn't going to hurt me to spend a little time doing this to help out. Ellie told me how important it is, with the ranch being short-handed and all. You're filling in, why can't I?"

"Why didn't you take the riding lesson this morning? Why aren't you out there with the other guests?"

Meg shrugged. "I didn't feel like it, that's all."

"You haven't done much of anything with the others," he pointed out. "Why did you come to the Triple B, anyway, if you don't like doing the sort of things we offer?"

Meg felt the noose she'd made for herself grow tighter. It was time to think like Margaret Chastain. "Because my aunt gave me this vacation as a gift," she fibbed. "She wanted me to experience something different."

"Different," he repeated, as if the word held some special meaning. "And this is so different. You in here doing what you do when you're not on vacation." His gaze met hers, daring her to deny it.

Meg didn't know whether to be exasperated by his concern or pleased that he cared. "I give up," she said, moving past him to the door. "You obviously don't want my help, and you can't understand why I offered it."

At the door, she stopped. Gazing at his wide shoulders, so set in defense and anger, she wished she could tell him the truth. But she couldn't. "If it will make you any happier, I told Janet Henderson that I would go with her and her husband later. Ted's going to teach me how to fish. So I do want to be involved like everyone else."

Without waiting to hear his reaction, she left the house, not sure that she cared what he might have to say.

"Way to go, Brannigan," Trey muttered. "You can't figure the woman out, so you make her mad."

He hadn't meant to do it, but damn, he didn't want to see her spending her time playing secretary. And she'd done such a good job of it, too. One look at the usually messy ranch office, and he knew Ellie had been right—they should have replaced Sherry a long time ago. But it had never been the right time. Trey had his hands full with making sure the dude part of the ranch was running properly and worrying if the Triple B was pleasing the guests. Everything had to be perfect. Especially now with *Trail's End* looking them over. He wanted nothing more than to prove to Chace and Dev that he could make a success of the dude ranch they'd both been dead set against.

"She did a good job, didn't she?"

Trey turned to see Ellie in the doorway. "Yeah, I guess she did," he admitted, feeling even worse. He sure hadn't told Meg he was pleased.

"Maybe we could talk her into staying," Ellie said, coming into the room and settling on his dad's old wing-back chair.

"What do you mean?"

Ellie shrugged. "It's just that…well, she seemed to enjoy herself today. More…I don't know. Animated? Not so closed off?"

"We'll find somebody for the job. Until then, we'll

deal with it," he said, moving to the chair behind the desk and easing down onto it.

Ellie studied him, her brow wrinkled. "But you'd think she'd want to get away from work. Maybe she isn't happy where she is. Has she ever mentioned her job?"

"I never asked her," he replied. "It never came up."

Ellie shot him a mischievous grin. "Why doesn't that surprise me?"

Trey wasn't certain why it had embarrassed him to be caught with Meg earlier. It wasn't as if Ellie or anybody else had never found him lavishing his attention on a woman. In fact, if all the ribbing he took was any indication, most everybody expected it of him.

"She's got us on the right track, it looks like," he said, ignoring Ellie's jab. "No reason we can't take it from here."

"But we need someone like Meg all the time," Ellie insisted. "She knows what she's doing. She's the kind of person who can make a difference." Scooting to the edge of the chair, Ellie became more animated. "I listened to her talking to prospective guests. Trey, she was great! Being a guest herself, she could honestly give her answers from a guest's viewpoint. And unlike Sherry, she has an enthusiasm I doubt anyone around here could match."

"So you're suggesting we hire her?" Trey asked, laughing. "She's on vacation, Ellie. You know, those things we never get to take?" he added with a wry smile. "What makes you think she'd quit what might be a perfectly good job to come work here on the Triple B?"

Ellie looked him square in the eye. "You."

Trey's next breath caught in his chest. "Me?" he said, barely able to get the word out. He shook his head to recover from the surprise she'd given him. "Just because you saw me with my arm around her doesn't mean she'd give up a life she knows and come to live here."

"Wouldn't you like to get to know her better?"

Would he? He hadn't given it much thought. Mostly, he just figured she'd be leaving at the end of the week, and that would be the end of it. But something more lasting? It wasn't what he'd planned, that's for sure. But he hadn't completely come to terms with the fact that she really would be leaving, either.

He pushed away from the desk and stood. Walking over to where Ellie sat smiling up at him, he tweaked her nose. "You know, sister-in-law, I really do like you. But sometimes, you let your romantic notions get the better of you. There's nothing going on between Miz Margaret Chastain and me that hasn't gone on with a hundred others."

"She's nothing special?" Ellie asked as he turned to leave the room.

He stopped. Special? He sure as hell couldn't say she wasn't.

He pulled off his hat and raked his fingers through his hair. "No. I mean, yes." He shook his head. "Hell, I don't know what I mean."

"If you're that unsure, Trey, maybe you'd better find out."

Trey wasn't so sure he wanted to do that. Something told him that this woman, who was getting to him bit by bit, might be dangerous to his well-being. And he wasn't ready for that. He didn't figure he ever would be.

Still, he was curious. "So what do you suggest?"

"I think you should ask her if she might be interested in taking a job at the Triple B. Find out if she's happy with her current job, or if she might want to try something different."

It didn't take long for Trey to consider it. Did he really want Meg around? Indefinitely? Living here, or even nearby? It solved the problem of not seeing her again after Sunday. And he had to admit, there was a part of him that wasn't looking forward to saying goodbye. But what about two or three months from now? What would happen when the excitement wore off, the way it always did, and they were stuck working together? It didn't sound good to Trey. Not good at all.

"If you won't ask her, I will," Ellie said, breaking into his thoughts.

Trey knew Ellie could be stubborn. From the stories Chace told about when the two of them first met, Trey knew that once Ellie got an idea in her head, she wouldn't let go. "Whose ranch is this?" he asked, hoping to lead her in another direction.

"It's yours and Dev's and Chace's." Lifting her chin, defiance flashed in her eyes. "And mine, too. But this is for the good of the ranch, Trey. You're not going to find anybody more willing to help than Meg. And with the talent she's shown, she'd be a gem for the ranch."

Trey couldn't deny it, if what Ellie had said earlier was true. "How many reservations did she book?"

Ellie stood, walked to the desk, and flipped the reservation book open. "About a dozen," she said, looking through the pages. "And she wrote down all of the information on each one so we can do a follow-up call if you think we need to." She turned to face him. "But I was here for part of them, and I know she did exactly what you and I would do. Even better."

Twelve reservations in a day? Trey couldn't believe it. They usually felt lucky if they had half a dozen in a week. "All right," he gave in. "I'll ask her. But don't count on it, okay?"

Nodding, Ellie grinned. "And if she says no, ask her if it'd be possible for her to stay an extra week or two until we can hire someone else. We really do need her, Trey."

"Yeah, yeah."

Trey sat reasoning with himself after Ellie left. He wasn't hot on the idea of having Meg here for any length of time. But it wasn't Meg. It was him. He knew his track record. He wasn't the type of man to settle down with one woman. He left that to Chace. And he pretty much had it figured out that Meg was a forever kind of woman, the kind he steered clear of. He didn't want to see her hurt. But the Triple B sure could stand having her around for a while.

The question was, how could he approach her with this job offer and not come off like some unfeeling jerk, yet still not promise her anything permanent? He wasn't sure, but he did know that he had to find a way. Somehow. If only for the good of the Triple B.

Chapter Six

An air of festivity filled the night as Meg made her way from her cottage to the campfire. For the occasion, the activities had been moved to behind the main ranch house, instead of in front of it. When she turned the corner of the house, her breath caught at what she knew was the culmination of a busy day for many of the staff. Miniature white lights were strung in the trees and along the hand-hewn fence surrounding the patio, giving everything a fairyland quality. A long trailer stood just to the side of the campfire and was occupied by a group of musicians who were in the midst of tuning their instruments and adjusting their equipment. As she drew nearer, she saw that a wooden dance floor had been added to the grassy yard that sprawled out wide before the ground dipped to the more rugged countryside she knew took over farther out.

Tugging at her dress, Meg nearly turned back to hide away in her cottage. She had almost not come to the evening's activity. Her emotions were in turmoil. She didn't particularly want to face Trey, and she had a feeling he didn't want to face her, either. Not after his hot and cold treatment over the past couple of days. She knew she should be thankful for the cold part of it, but it was the hot part that bothered her the most.

She chose to take her place at the edge of the larger than usual group of guests and ranch hands, and stood in the shadows where she hoped she wouldn't be noticed. The band soon broke into a rousing country number she vaguely recognized. One of the other writers on the magazine was a country music fan, but Meg was usually too engrossed in her work to notice. The song was a real toe tapper though, and she found herself caught up in the tune.

Ellie joined her, clapping her hands along with the others. "Looks like everyone is enjoying themselves already. Except you."

"I'm having a good time. Really," Meg answered.

"Hiding away here in the dark?" Ellie shook her head. "I know you're shy, but come join the rest of the guests."

Guilt nagged at Meg. Had she really not joined in with the others, as Trey had said? She had meant to fade into the background, but instead, had she stuck out as the antisocial one? She hoped not.

"You all do such a wonderful job," Meg assured her. "I've seen the extra little touches the staff take with each guest." She nearly said that noticing those things was a part of her job, but she caught herself in time.

"I hope all the guests are as appreciative as you are," Ellie said.

Chace approached them to join his wife and Ellie introduced Meg to him. "He's been so busy getting ready for the trail ride, we've hardly seen each other."

With only the twinkling lights for illumination, and with his hat pulled low, Meg wasn't able to see Chace well, but something about him was familiar. "I wouldn't have thought a trail ride would take so much time and attention."

"It wouldn't," Chace answered, "except this isn't just a trail ride. We need to move some of the herd off the pasture land where they've been grazing, and onto some that hasn't been touched yet this season. That takes the efforts of everyone."

Even though she'd done her research, Meg hadn't completely understood the term "working ranch" until now. "I hadn't realized it was a real part of the ranch work," she told them both, "even though I'd read the brochure. I started thinking about it when I was taking reservations, but now I understand."

Ellie looked up at her husband and smiled. "We're not the only dude ranch, or even working dude ranch, in the Banderas. We just want to be the best."

Meg couldn't miss the pride in the ranch both of them shared. Or the love they shared for each other when Chace put his arm around his wife and drew her closer. Meg's hopes were high that the Triple B would gain popularity, but she also hoped she could write her review with objectivity, now that she'd gotten to know so many of the staff.

"How about some two-steppin', Little Bit?" Chace asked his wife.

"I'd like that." Ellie turned to Meg. "Will you be okay by yourself?"

"I'll be fine," Meg assured her. "You two go enjoy yourselves. I'll just watch. Maybe I can learn something."

She watched them take their places along with the others, fascinated by their intricate dance steps. Across the way, she could see Trey threading his way through the crowd in her direction. Was he running hot tonight, or cold? she wondered.

"Trying to hide from me?" he asked when he came to a stop in front of her.

By the charming grin he wore, Meg knew she was in trouble. Trey was definitely running hot. The spark in his eyes affirmed it.

"I don't have any reason to hide," she answered as her heartbeat drummed in her chest. She couldn't let her hormones direct her actions. Somehow, she had to find a way to keep his sexy smile from getting to her.

"Good." He moved to stand beside her, taking her hand and lacing his fingers with hers. "I thought they'd never leave."

Meg cautioned herself to ignore the flutter in her heart, but the surge of excitement at his touch was impossible to fight. "That sounds like an old movie line," she said, hoping to discourage any more.

Trey chuckled. "Yeah, I guess it did. I was afraid you were mad at me."

The warmth of her hand, wrapped in his, overshadowed the panic she was feeling. "Why would I be angry?" she asked, doing her best to dismiss the way her heart fluttered each time he spoke.

Trey touched her cheek with one finger, turning her face to him, and gazed into her eyes. "Don't know, except I was kinda hard on you in the office today. I'm sorry, Meg. Forgive me?"

Her resolve to remain aloof began to weaken. "There's nothing to forgive. For whatever reason, you're very protective of the ranch. I can't fault that."

"It's not that. I want you to enjoy yourself, not spend your vacation working," he said, letting his finger trail down her cheek to rest at the pulse point below her ear.

"I—I am," she answered, her voice breathless. If only she could get her knees to feel more substantial than melted butter. The man must think she was an absolute pushover, the way she seemed to dissolve at his touch.

His smile didn't do much to lend her any strength. "Why don't we join the others," he suggested, tipping his head in the direction of the dance floor.

Meg noticed that the snappy number the band had been playing was now replaced with a slow song. Dancing with him might not be a good idea, especially since she wasn't sure how much longer she could even stand. "Maybe you should go ahead." But when she tried to step away from him, he stopped her.

"I need a dance partner, sweetheart. I'll look pretty silly out there all by myself."

Tugging on the hand he held, he led her to the dance floor and turned her into his arms. The trembling in her knees matched the one in her hands, and she wasn't sure exactly where she should put them. Everybody else dancing had theirs in all different positions. Trey, however, didn't seem to have a problem with his as he tightened them around her and pulled her closer.

"Relax, Meg. I won't bite you right here in front of everybody."

She tried for a smile. "I didn't think you would." It wasn't a fear of being bitten that was troubling her. It was her fear that he might decide to kiss her. If it was anything like the last time, she might not live through it. Especially with an audience. She settled for placing her hands on the curve of his strong shoulders, and hoped it would be the perfect position if she needed to put him in his place.

She could feel him watching her, and finally gave in to the pull of his gaze to look up. It was the wrong thing to do. Trey's eyes held promises for more than she'd bargained for. More than she needed to let herself in for.

"Have you ever thought of contacts?" he asked, slipping her glasses off and putting them in his shirt pocket. "You have the most beautiful eyes."

Meg felt herself blush. She'd heard other men say the same thing, but it sounded different coming from Trey. As though he was sincere. And then she realized that, once again, she'd let his words go straight to her heart. Why should she believe him when she'd never believed anyone else?

"Thank you," she answered, dipping her head to stare at the pocket where her glasses now resided.

Pulling her even closer, so their bodies were pressed together, he whispered in her ear. "Can you see me without them?"

She fell for the trick, looking up again, and wanted to kick herself. He was so close, his breath whispered across her cheek. "Well enough to know that you're too close."

Instead of backing off, he grinned. "You don't like slow dancing?"

"It's not the dancing," she tried to explain, "it's just that you're…"

"Too close." He put an inch more of space between them. "If it makes you that uncomfortable, I can offer something a little different."

Her interest was raised. "What might that be?"

The muscles in his shoulder moved beneath her hands as he shrugged. "A ride. The moon is bright enough tonight that we shouldn't have any trouble navigating. And I owe you a ride, since you gave up your class this morning to lend a hand in the office."

She wasn't sure it was a good idea to be alone with him, but she decided it couldn't get too cozy if they were riding on separate horses. "That sounds wonderful," she agreed with a smile.

Before he released her, his hands slid down her back, causing a tremble to follow it. "Great. Besides, I need to talk to you about something." Keeping one arm around her, he guided her in the direction of the barn.

Meg wasn't so sure she'd made the right decision while she watched Trey saddle and ready two horses. She was leaving Sunday, and if she could just keep that in mind, maybe she'd be safe. The problem was, she had trouble remembering much of anything when she was around him. But she was curious to know what he wanted to talk to her about.

* * *

A moonlight ride was a spur-of-the-moment idea Trey hoped he wouldn't regret. Holding Meg on the makeshift dance floor had been almost more than he could take. Like her, he'd needed to put some distance between them. If he hadn't, he was afraid he wouldn't have been able to keep from doing something he might never live down. He'd kissed women in front of people before, but Meg was a guest. Just dancing with her, holding her close, was risking censure. And he wasn't sure how Emery might take it. The Triple B sure didn't need their rating knocked down just because he couldn't keep his hands to himself when he was around this woman.

After Trey made sure Meg was mounted, they made their way out of the barn and headed into the moonlit night, leaving the music behind.

"Ellie told me to be sure and listen to Theresa's husband sing," Meg said as the sounds of a George Strait tune drifted to a whisper.

"Miguel called earlier to say he had a heifer that's ready to calf on his hands. He'll be here later, if he can. Maybe you'll still get a chance to hear him."

"I'd like that."

Trey took his time, studying her as they rode side by side. He knew the ranch so well, he could have ridden it blindfolded. And he knew exactly where he was taking her.

"You ride pretty good," he told her after they hadn't spoken for several minutes.

Meg ducked her head before glancing at him. "I'm surprised I caught on so quickly."

"You really did take to it," Trey said when she turned to look at him. "You might have had trouble mounting that first day, and forgot to keep your heels down, but you weren't nervous like most people are their first time on a horse."

"Sure I was. You just didn't notice." She paused a moment, then cleared her throat. "I've heard cowboys tend to wander, but you said you'd been here most of your life."

"Some do," he answered, taking his time. He knew there were men who couldn't settle down on a ranch or anywhere else. He'd never been like that. He'd kept his rodeo riding close to home. The ranch had been too important to him, even then, to be away from it for long. He knew Chace had strong feelings for the ranch, too. But the need for money, and possessing more talent than Trey had ever hoped to have, had kept his brother traveling on the circuit.

He wondered if there was something in Meg's past that brought out her caution around him. Or maybe she was just cautious around all men. That might account for her strange wardrobe. "Doesn't sound like you think much of cowboys."

Her smile was sweet when she looked at him. "To be honest, you're the first I've ever met."

Taking a deep breath, he let it out slowly. "Like I said, some cowboys like to roam, but not all cowboys are like that. Look at Chace."

"Ellie is a very lucky woman."

He didn't have a reply. His brother had lucked out and married a woman who suited him. But Trey had never been that lucky. Or maybe he had been, since he had never considered settling down. He might be a cowboy who stayed in one place, whose family came before everything, but he didn't have any intentions of adding to that family with a wife of his own. He'd always said that because ranching kept him tied to one spot, he liked women to provide him with the variety he craved. And he hadn't had anything to complain about yet.

So why did he feel this attraction to the woman riding beside him? Even more than an attraction. She wasn't anything like the women he dated. He was stumped at what it was that made him want to hold her close and feel her heart beat with his.

He figured he'd brought her on this ride for a lot of reasons. One, dancing with her just wasn't enough. Two, he wanted to spend some time with her. Knowing she'd be leaving soon made him uneasy. And three, he wanted to present Ellie's idea in the best light he could, which meant the darker the better. He wanted her to stay. Not forever, but for longer than a few days. He wasn't sure how he would react to her answer, whatever she decided. Darkness provided a cover of safety.

And it was time.

When he cleared his throat, ready to do the deed, the sound seemed almost deafening in the silence of the night. He ignored it and forced himself to continue. "Ellie's real impressed with what you did today. I am, too."

Meg shrugged. "I only answered the phone and filed a few papers. Nothing more than a good receptionist or secretary would do."

"Yeah, well, I won't argue with you about that," he

admitted. In one afternoon, she had done more than Sherry had even thought of doing in a month. "But it won't be easy finding somebody who's as good as you."

Meg's laughter rang out in the darkness. "Oh, I doubt that. I'm sure if you look around, it won't be long before you find someone. Probably someone better."

He disagreed, but he didn't argue. If they were lucky enough to find someone with Meg's skill at enticing callers to make reservations, she wouldn't know beans about how to file a paper. And if she was a whiz at filing... No, nobody could do what Meg did. Not as far as he was concerned. Which gave him that much more reason to agree with Ellie and try to woo Meg to the Triple B. The only way to do that was to jump in with both feet and hope for the best.

"Are you happy with the job you have now?"

Meg sat up straighter in the saddle before she answered. "Yes, as a matter of fact, I am."

"So you wouldn't be interested in a change?"

She pulled up her horse and turned to stare at him. "What do you mean?"

Trey shrugged. "Ellie and I thought— Well, it was Ellie's idea, but we thought you might be willing to come work at the Triple B."

Her mouth opened, then closed, and she shook her head, as if she wasn't sure she was hearing him right. "You mean you're suggesting that I stay?"

"Well, yeah, I am." He waited to let the idea sink in before adding, "You were terrific today. That's the kind of thing the ranch needs to put it on top. We all work together here to make the Triple B a success. You fit right in."

She didn't seem to hear him. "You mean you want me to go back home and pack up my things and just move down here?"

His hopes hit his boots. Up ahead, he could see the creek shimmering silver in the moonlight. He'd planned to make his offer in a more enticing way, but things had just seemed to get out of hand. He'd blown it by not sticking to his plan.

"I guess it is asking a lot, especially if you're happy doing whatever it is you do," he admitted. "By the way, you've never said what kind of work you do."

She twisted the end of the reins around her finger and didn't look at him. "I work in an office."

"They must be real happy to have you."

She nodded. "Yeah, I guess they are."

Trey urged his horse forward, watching to make sure Meg followed. When she did, he led her down an incline to the creek and stopped. Dismounting, he reached up and offered her his hand. Pulling her left foot from the stirrup, she swung her other leg over the horse's neck and slid to the ground with his help.

"It's beautiful," she said with a sigh when they reached the edge of the creek.

"One of the prettiest spots on the Triple B," he agreed. "But not the only one." He turned her to face him and tipped her chin up to look at him. "There's you, for one." Lowering his head, he pressed his lips to hers, savoring the soft sweetness he'd come to crave. But he didn't linger. "If you stayed for a while, I could show you more."

"I—I don't know, Trey."

He slipped his arms around her and looked down into her eyes. "Ellie thought maybe you might be willing to stay for a couple of weeks. If you could take the time off from your job, that is."

She shook her head. "I can't do that." She placed her hand against his cheek. "I'd like to help. I really would. But my job isn't just a place where I work from nine to five. It's my career. It's the most important thing in my life."

"Even more important than—" He'd wanted to ask if it was more important than he was, but he stopped himself. Considering the fact that he wasn't offering her anything permanent—at least not with him—he was a fool for even thinking it. "Even more important than people?"

Nodding, Meg smiled. "There's no one else. There isn't time for anyone. This vacation is the only time I've taken off in years."

"And here we had you working on your vacation," he said, shaking his head and feeling even worse that they had taken advantage of her generosity.

"I enjoyed it, Trey. When are you going to understand that?"

"Never, I guess," he said with a chuckle to cover his disappointment. "Although I suppose if I had a vacation, I'd probably spend it at a rodeo or something. But if you should change your mind— Not that we're pushing or anything." He added a grin to ease the tension, and Meg's smile grew wider.

"I don't think I will, but you never know, right?"

"Right."

Before he had a chance to steal another kiss, she pulled away. "If we hurry back, maybe we can catch Miguel."

Trey squashed the sigh that welled up in him at the thought of returning. But the disappointment at her refusal was even bigger. A kiss or two wasn't going to change things. The Triple B would get along just fine without Meg. They still had Richard Emery's rating in *Trail's End* to give them a boost. Trey was going to make sure everything went right so they'd get a good review. And they'd find a new secretary. She might not live up to what Meg had done, but he doubted anyone would.

Besides, it was better this way. He wasn't planning on making a commitment and was sure that, in a matter of time, he would've regretted asking Meg to stay. But he had a feeling it would take a little longer than it usually did to move on to the next little darlin' that caught his eye.

Meg awakened the next morning filled with guilt. She hadn't expected that her deception would bother her when she'd set out from the magazine's office in Chicago to get the interview of a lifetime. But it did. She had been forced to lie too many times. She'd had to lead Trey into believing she was someone she wasn't. If he ever found out who she really was— Well, it didn't bear thinking about. She had been working on the review and knew it was good. Nearly everything at the Triple B was exceptional. She couldn't think of one bad thing to say about the ranch. Especially considering that they were two ranch hands short and their secretary had quit, causing everyone to take on extra duties. And she hadn't heard one complaint. Not from the staff or the guests.

After she'd dressed, she hurried to the chuckwagon to join the other guests for breakfast. Today was the day she'd planned to talk with them and get their opinions of the Triple B.

"If it's okay, I'll skip the class today," she told Ellie when they met at the breakfast buffet.

Ellie smiled. "Trey said your riding is coming along fine. I think everybody's is, from what I've seen."

"It's because we have such a great teacher."

Her cheeks reddening, Ellie ducked her head. "I think it's because I have such a great bunch of students." They sat together at the table, across from the Hendersons, who were discussing the trail ride.

"I hope I'll be able to walk by Sunday," Janet Henderson said with a wry smile.

"There'll be plenty of chances to rest and walk around," Ellie assured her. "It's about a four-hour ride. You'll start out early because of the heat, but Chace and Trey will stop several times so you can all rest and walk around."

"And then we'll come back on Sunday morning?" Janet's husband Ted asked.

Ellie nodded. "Part of the fun is cooking over an open fire and roughing it. It's not the same as the campfires we have here. No soft bed to sleep in when you're ready to drop. No hot shower to ease the aches and pains. But if you don't enjoy it, I'll eat my saddle blanket," she said with a grin. Standing, she picked up her plate. "And speaking of saddle blankets, I need to go get one on Sky Dancer. I'll be doing some barrel racing as part of our rodeo exhibition later."

Janet nodded eagerly. "We're looking forward to watching it. I know that both you and your husband were rodeo professionals."

"It keeps us in shape," Ellie said with a grin and a shrug before she left them.

Janet turned to Meg. "We're really enjoying this vacation," she said. "It's so different than anything we've ever done."

"She had to talk me into it," Ted said, putting his arm around his wife. "It sounded too much like that Billy Crystal movie to me, but it's been very relaxing."

"Ted's an air traffic controller," Janet explained. "He needed to get out in the open and enjoy something completely different. That's why we enjoyed our little fishing expedition yesterday."

Meg smiled. "I enjoyed it, too. And everything else. This is the first time I've ever been on a horse. It's made me realize there's a lot more to life than work."

Later, standing along the fence around the corral, Meg looked back on the past four days, feeling like she had accomplished most of what she had been sent to the Triple B to do. Today's mini-rodeo and the next day and night's trail ride were the big events of the week, but as far as she was concerned, the Triple B had proven its worth. As long as she could still manage to stay objective about it, and she was doing a good job of that in spite of Trey, she wouldn't have a problem with the review and article.

Ellie's riding amazed Meg. For someone who hadn't competed for almost two years, the diminutive woman could still handle a horse with precision. The other guests were as impressed as Meg was, and not only with Ellie, but with her husband and the other hands who performed, as well. When it was all over and the dust settled, the applause from the small group of spectators was more than appreciative.

She watched as Trey thanked everyone. The other guests wandered away in small groups, but Meg decided to stay and see what was up. She'd noticed that Richard Emery hadn't left with the others, and that two of the ranch hands were leading a horse into the chute where Chace and another cowboy had mounted the broncs they'd ridden. When Trey waved Emery over to the chute, Meg's curiosity grew. What were they planning? Surely Richard Emery wasn't going to attempt to ride that horse.

Transfixed, Meg couldn't move. She'd spoken to Emery in passing several times, and the man struck her as being hardly what anyone would call athletic. He had done fairly well in the riding class, but then both Trey and Ellie had taken a little more time with him than they had with anyone else. Meg was certain it was because the staff all believed Emery was the reporter from *Trail's End.* She couldn't blame them for doing their best to impress him. Anyone else would have done the same thing in their position. Wasn't that exactly why she was in disguise? But letting Richard Emery get on a bucking horse was taking it a bit too far.

Meg held her breath, her hands gripping the fence rails in front of her as she watched the man climb into the chute. Frantic that he might be hurt doing such a foolish thing, she looked around for Trey. Maybe, she hoped, she could talk him into putting a stop to this crazy idea. But Trey had disappeared, and Pete seemed to be in charge.

She watched in horror as Richard Emery mounted the horse. Two cowboys on either side of him had climbed on the sides of the chute and were helping him twist the rope around his hand. They jumped out of the way when Emery nodded, and the gate was pulled open.

The horse charged into the corral, kicking his rear legs in the air while Emery held on with one hand, his other waving in the air. It occurred to Meg that the horse wasn't as wild as the ones the hands had ridden earlier, but it wasn't a Sunday ride in the country, either. When one of the cowboys let out a loud whistle, the horse bucked even more, sending Emery flying into the air to land in the dust.

Meg was livid. Climbing the fence in spite of the fact that the bronc was still loose inside the corral, she stomped toward Pete while the other ranch hands circled the horse to lead it away from the downed rider. Without giving it much thought, she saw that the horse had calmed and was meekly allowing one of the cowboys to loop a rope around its neck. It didn't stop her or slow her down.

"Are you in charge?" she asked Pete, planting her balled fists on her hips.

Pete looked around as if she were talking to someone else. Tipping his hat back on his head, he grinned. "Why, no, ma'am. I'm not."

Her patience was wearing thin. "Look, someone has to be in charge. If it's not you, then who is it?"

"Trey's in charge, Miz Chastain."

She should have been surprised, but she wasn't. Hadn't she seen Trey involved in most of the ranch work? "And where is Trey?"

"I reckon he went with Chace to check out the trail for tomorrow. They won't be back for a while."

"Like how long?" she demanded.

Pete shrugged in that easy cowboy way that Meg was beginning to hate more each moment. "Sometime late this afternoon, I reckon."

"This afterno—" Meg threw her hands in the air, then hurried over to check on Richard Emery, who was limping toward the fence. "Mr. Emery, are you all right?"

He turned to look at her, rubbing an elbow with one hand and holding his bent wire-rimmed glasses in the other. "Why, of course, I am, Miss Chastain," he said with a smile. "Thank you for your concern, however."

Meg blew like an overstocked steam engine. "Are you nuts? Getting on a crazy horse like that? You could have been killed. Why did you agree to do it?"

Emery's smile was on the verge of condescending. "I didn't agree, Miss Chastain. Nobody asked me to ride that bronc. I asked them if they'd let me try."

"Then you're as crazy as they are," she snapped. "Even crazier, since these men have a clue as to what they're risking if they do it. I intend to take this up with the person in charge." Whirling around to make her way back to her cottage, she muttered under her breath, "As soon as the dumb cowboy gets back."

Chapter Seven

"I sure hated telling Ellie that Meg wouldn't come to work for us," Trey told Chace. They'd been riding for a good hour, and he was glad that the ranch was in sight.

Chace nodded. "She was disappointed, but I think she probably figured all along that Meg wouldn't stay. I'm wondering how you're taking the news, though." He turned to Trey with a grin.

"Me? I'm taking it fine, I guess," Trey said, feeling odd. "Why wouldn't I?"

Chace stared into the distance, squinting into the sun. "It's pretty obvious you've taken a liking to her."

Laughing, Trey shook his head. "I take a liking to a lot of women. You know that."

"I got the feeling Meg was kind of different, though."

Even though he knew his brother wasn't even looking at him, Trey was beginning to feel like a bug under a microscope. "Well, she is, I guess," he managed to answer. "But maybe that's why I'm interested right now."

"So you admit that you're interested."

"Hell, Chace. Interested doesn't mean I'm gonna run off and marry her," Trey pointed out. "It's just that, yeah, she is different."

"So was Ellie."

Trey smiled, thinking of his sister-in-law. "She still is."

They rode for several minutes before Chace spoke again. "You know, I almost lost her."

"Sure," Trey said, remembering the stories he'd heard about how the two had met and eventually married. "She almost married J.R. and then you rescued her."

Chace chuckled. "If only it had been that easy. No, it was because I didn't want to admit that I loved her. Sometimes that's the hardest part."

"Some men have trouble saying it," Trey said with a shrug. "Personally, I've never felt the need to," he added with a grin and a wink.

"Now, see, that's where you're getting confused, little brother. It wasn't that I wouldn't tell her. It was that I wouldn't admit it to myself." He gave Trey a sideways look. "Sound familiar?"

"Nope, it sure doesn't," Trey stated with certainty.

"Uh-huh."

"You think I wouldn't know if some little darlin' had snagged my heart?" Trey shook his head at the foolish idea. "Fact is, not one of them ever has. And not one of them ever will, far as I can see."

"Damn, Trey, you're as stubborn as Ellie."

Reining in his horse, Trey stopped and regarded his

brother with a long look. "Did your wife suggest this little talk?"

Chace shook his head as he came to a stop, too. "Nope. But Ellie did mention that she thought there was more going on than it looks like. Just so happens that I agree with her."

Trey wondered if there wasn't something to it. Not love, just… There didn't seem to be a word for it. When it came to Meg Chastain, he'd never been more confused in his life. "Okay," he said, urging his horse into a walk again, "there is something kind of fascinating about Meg. Don't ask me what it is. I've been trying to figure it out."

"Sounds like you've spent some time on it," Chace commented.

"Hell, yes, I have. It's been driving me nuts."

"But you're gonna keep on denying it until it's too late, aren't you?"

"Look, I admit she's gettin' to me. But it's not love. No way," Trey said, determined to get it across to his brother. "She'll be going home on Sunday and that'll be the end of it." For some odd reason, just saying it left him with an empty feeling. But he wasn't going to give in to it.

"Yep. That's the same way I thought with Ellie," Chace told him. "I stopped in at her hotel room to tell her goodbye and wish her luck the night before the last round." He pulled his hat lower as if he wanted to hide, and when he moved in the saddle, the leather creaked beneath him. "Thought she was marrying Jimmy Bob, and when I walked out of that room after turning down her offer of— Anyway, I can remember thinking there was nothing left to do. I pretty well gave up."

"You'd have gone after her if you hadn't found her here at the ranch when you got back," Trey pointed out, knowing the story well.

Chace nodded, his mouth set in a firm line. "Yeah, but there's no telling what would have happened. If Ellie wasn't so stubborn, she wouldn't have come here looking for me. I might not have found her." He turned to look at Trey. "Then where would I be?"

Trey gave it some thought. "I see your point, but it's not the same."

"Course not," Chace agreed. "Meg isn't the type to come back."

Trey knew better than to argue. He wasn't in love with Meg Chastain. She would be leaving Sunday, and that would be the end of it. No pining for a woman for him. He wasn't the marrying kind, and no woman could change that.

But Chace's words haunted him as they rode into the yard, and he couldn't forget them as they stabled their horses.

When the brothers emerged from the barn, the first thing Trey did was look for Meg. He grinned when he saw her headed toward him. But his smile dimmed as she got closer. Something was wrong. Really wrong.

She stopped in front of him and he couldn't miss the bright spots of color on her cheeks. "I hear you're in charge," she said, poking a finger at his chest and backing him up two steps.

Chace sidestepped the action and tipped his hat to Meg. "I'm outta here."

But she didn't seem to hear. Her fury was directed at

Trey. He didn't have a clue what the problem was, but he had a feeling he was going to find out.

"Did it ever occur to you that Richard Emery could have broken his neck? What would that have done for the Triple B?" She poked him one more time, but he refused to budge. "Huh? Tell me."

Trey wrapped his hand around her finger, pulled her hand away and didn't let go. "What's this all about? Emery's bronc ride this morning?"

"Of course it's about the bronc ride," she said, her voice rising. "The man was a fool to ask if he could do it, but if you allowed it, you're an even bigger fool."

"Listen, Meg—"

"No, you listen, mister. I hold you responsible for this, but you can bet your spurs that I'm going to let the owner know how irresponsible you've been."

"Meg, that horse—"

"That horse could have killed that man," she finished for him.

He dropped her hand and placed his hands on her shoulders, hoping to calm her. When she tried to pull away, he held her more firmly. "Will you cool off and listen to me?"

"Maybe I should just tell Chace Brannigan right now," she said, ignoring him. "I'm sure he didn't know what was going on around here. He's a sensible man. Unlike you."

"Meg, honey, you don't know anything about what was going on," Trey insisted.

"I know that Chace Brannigan is one of the owners of this ranch. He and his two brothers."

Trey nodded. "That's right. Chace, Dev and me."

"And if I can't get any satisfaction—" She stopped. The bright spots of color disappeared from her cheeks, along with most of the color. If there had been a strong wind, it would've knocked her over. "You? What do you mean? The third brother's name is Buford."

With a groan, he dropped his chin to his chest. Raising his head, he pulled his hat lower and looked around to make sure no one was within hearing range. Settling his gaze on her, he kept his voice low. "Don't make a big announcement of it, okay?"

"*You're* Buford?"

"You didn't know that?"

She stood completely still for a moment and finally shook her head.

"Buford Brannigan was my granddaddy," he explained when she didn't say anything. "My daddy was Buford Junior, but everybody called him Buck. He was able to hold off on giving Chace and Dev his name until I came along. My mama had always insisted that she wanted one son to carry his name. I guess he finally got tired of fighting her on it, because he agreed, as long as they called me Trey. It means 'three'."

Meg nodded and found her tongue. "I know that. Obviously your father was a poker player."

Trey grinned. She was sharper than he sometimes gave her credit for. "So was my mama. Now, if you'll let me explain about that ride—"

"A very dangerous ride," she said, and seemed to regain some of the equilibrium she had lost. "I still can't believe you let him do it."

"He wasn't in danger," Trey told her. "That was a broke horse. The boys tightened the cinch to make him buck a little, that's all. And he didn't buck much, I'd bet on it."

"But that's not the point," she argued. "He could have been badly hurt. Then where would the Triple B be? You'd have a lawsuit on your hands."

"Not with a signed release from Emery stating that we wouldn't be held responsible."

Meg blinked once, then twice. "You had him sign a waiver?"

"I'm no dummy, sweetheart. Of course I did. If common sense hadn't told me to do it, the business degree I have from UTSA would."

"Business degree?" Meg said, her voice weak.

Before he could tell her how he had worked the ranch while getting his education, they were interrupted.

"Phone call for Miz Chastain," Pete called as he hurried toward them from the house.

Meg's eyes widened and she pulled away.

"Wait a second," Trey said, grabbing her hand to stop her. "You're not mad that I'm part owner of the Triple B, are you?"

Shaking her head, she kept her gaze on the house behind him. "Just surprised, that's all."

"Okay," he said as he released her.

Without saying another word or even looking at him, she hurried up to the house. Trey watched her, wondering why she had acted so strangely when he had told her that he was Buford. He had to shake off the aversion he always felt when he thought about how his mother had saddled him with the name. Still, he was proud to be named after his granddad and daddy. If they had managed with it, he could, too.

And he wondered who might be calling Meg at the ranch. Whoever it was, he suspected it might be some kind of emergency. She had looked pretty rattled. Maybe it was something he could help her with. But he would have to wait until later. Chace was expecting him to help get everything ready for the trail ride in the morning. He would have to find Meg later to discover what had her so shook up.

Meg stepped inside the cool, dark interior of the house and hurried down the long hallway to the office. She knew Geraldine would call her on the cell phone she had brought along. The only other person it might be was Aunt Dee. Meg had called her aunt the night before, but there'd been no answer. She hadn't worried. Her aunt often spent the evenings playing bridge with friends. But if Aunt Dee called the ranch, it could be serious.

"There you are," Ellie said when Meg pushed open the door to the office. "There's a call for you. Since I wasn't sure where you were, I suggested that you could call him back, but he said he'd wait."

"Thanks, Ellie." Meg took the phone and waited until Ellie had slipped out of the room before speaking. "This is Meg Chastain."

"Meg? John Jeffers here."

Her heart stopped. If her neighbor was calling all the way to Texas this late, it wasn't good. "Is something wrong?" she managed to ask, fear prickling her skin. "Is Aunt Dee all right?"

"Dee is fine, but I thought I should call you. Sadie Adams, down on the corner, and I took your aunt to the emergency clinic this afternoon."

"Oh, no," Meg cried softly and covered her mouth with her hand.

"Now, she's all right. She was just having a little trouble catching her breath. They gave her one of those inhalation treatments and a shot, and sent her home."

Helpless, so far away, Meg didn't know what to do. "Maybe I should come home," she said, uncertain.

"No need to do that," Mr. Jeffers assured her. "Dee's been resting, and she's feeling as good as new."

Meg seriously doubted that. Aunt Dee didn't know what "new" felt like. She'd battled asthma for so long, she didn't remember what it was like to take a deep, clear breath.

"You're certain she's breathing easier?" she asked, hoping for an affirmative answer.

"Yes. She has her pills and inhaler. And we're getting ready for a quiet evening of bridge here at her house. She won't have to leave the air-conditioning."

Still not convinced her aunt would be safe, Meg didn't have a choice but to give in. "Be sure the filter on the air purifier is clean. In fact, there's a brand new box of them in the kitchen cabinet by the door."

"I'll take care of it as soon as I'm off the phone. She didn't want me to call you, but I felt that you should know."

"I'm so glad you did," Meg said, her voice still shaky. "And if she has another attack, you call me again, no matter what she says. I have my cell phone, so you won't need to bother the staff." She quickly gave him the number, then waited while he wrote it down and repeated it to her. "That's it. Call me any time. I'll keep the phone with me. And Mr. Jeffers?"

"Yes?"

"Thank you for taking care of Aunt Dee."

"It's my pleasure. You just relax and enjoy yourself there at that ranch."

Meg thanked him again and hung up. The asthma attacks had become more frequent, and the doctor had told them it was the Gary air that provoked them. Meg had to get Aunt Dee away from the pollutants of the city, and the only way she could do it was to write the best darned article on the Triple B Ranch that Geraldine Martin had ever seen.

Meg managed to return to her cabin without running into Trey or anyone else. Still shook up by her discovery and the news of her aunt's latest attack, she sank onto the nearest chair, her head spinning. Knowing that Trey was the owner of the Triple B made all the difference in the world. Could she do an honest, unbiased review of the ranch without her feelings entering into it? She hoped she could. She'd always been sensible, had always let her head rule instead of her heart. She could do the same with her article for the magazine.

But how could she explain that she'd missed the boat completely on who the owners were? Now she doubted her ability to do anything. Was there more she'd missed? Had she been so swayed by a charming, sexy cowboy that her view of the ranch had been colored?

One thing she did know was that she was hot and tired. She checked the time, noting that it wasn't as late as she had thought. If she took a quick shower, she would have time to call Geraldine on the cell phone she kept tucked inside her suitcase. It was time to be honest with her boss. Geraldine would understand. She had to. And maybe she could offer some advice. Meg could only hope.

Stripping off her clothes in the bathroom, she yanked the wig from her head. Two more days and she'd be done with this crazy assignment.

Two more days and she'd be leaving the Triple B, and Trey, behind.

Her knees went weak at the thought. Hoping a shower would revive her and give her back her strength, she forced herself to think of nothing as she turned on the water. Stepping inside, she slid the glass shower door closed, feeling protected from the outside world. As the spray stung her body, the thoughts she'd fought off crept into her mind.

Believing Trey was a ranch hand had been a safety net for her. Weren't cowboys notoriously transient? He had told her he had lived there forever. Why hadn't she understood that he meant he'd lived on the ranch, not just somewhere around? The answer was simple. She'd decided the moment she'd set eyes on him that he was nothing more than a ranch hand.

To know that he was a part owner of one of the biggest ranches in Texas changed things. He was nothing like she had thought. He was a stable, successful man who made her heart beat triple time. And she was in big,

big trouble. Trey was the cowboy that she could no longer deny she was losing her heart to.

Trey sat at the oak table in the Triple B's kitchen, shoving a piece of the finest steak in Texas around on his plate.

"Are you feeling all right, Trey?" Ellie asked from the sink behind him.

Chace, sitting across the table from him, chuckled. "He's down in the dumps because Meg lit into him about Richard Emery's bronc ride."

Ellie placed a hand on Trey's shoulder. "She'll cool off. Do you know what the phone call was about? If I hadn't been so busy checking the equipment for the trail ride tomorrow, I'd have gone and talked to her."

Trey shook his head. It wasn't because Meg had been so angry with him. It was the look on her face when he'd told her he was one of the Brannigan brothers that had him worried. That and the phone call.

He twisted his head to look up at Ellie. "She didn't have a clue that Chace and I are brothers."

Ellie's eyes widened. "Really? I knew who you were the first time I laid eyes on you."

Trey nodded and returned his gaze to his barely touched plate of food. "And for some reason, it bothered her to find out that I was one of the owners."

"Why would it make any difference?" Chace asked, looking from Trey to his wife. "Except maybe to find out that she'd been necking with one of the biggest landowners in the state."

Trey's head snapped up at the mention of the possibility that she might be after something, and he saw his brother shoot a wink at his sister-in-law. "I never said she was *excited* about the news," he told them both. "I said she was bothered by it. Like she was in some kind of shock or something." He shook his head. "I don't understand it."

"Maybe she felt foolish," Ellie suggested, circling the table to take a seat next to Chace. "Maybe she was embarrassed, although I don't know why she would be."

"She was acting kind of strange, that's all."

"She didn't say anything else? No clue about what might be bothering her?"

"Not a thing." Trey pushed away from the table and stood, grabbing his plate and carrying it to the sink. "To be honest, she looked like she was going to be sick. And then she went to take that phone call. I think she was shook up over that, too. Maybe I should go check on her."

"Good idea," Chace said as Trey started for the door. "If she needs anything, come back and tell Ellie."

From the porch, Trey could see that the light in Meg's cabin was still on. He was worried. He hadn't been kidding when he'd said she looked like she might be sick. She'd been as pale as the palomino he'd picked out for her to ride that first morning.

What if she was sick? Or what if she was hurt? For a second, his heartbeat stopped, and then he bounded down the steps and rushed across the wide expanse between the house and the cabins. Fear squeezed at his heart. He tried to tell himself that he'd feel the same way about any one of the guests at the ranch, but he knew that wasn't true. He might be concerned about them, but he wouldn't feel the panic he was feeling at the thought of something happening to Meg.

Before he stepped onto her porch, he peered in the window for signs of her moving about. What he saw hit him like the hind legs of a bucking bronc.

Sitting in the chair, her feet propped on the table in front of her, Meg wore nothing more than a towel wrapped around her body, and another wrapped around her head. In her hand, she held a cellular phone against her ear. And she was smiling.

But it wasn't her smile that froze Trey to the spot. It was the body that was barely covered by one of the Triple B guest towels. From her slender shoulders and the enticing cleavage that peeked over the edge of the towel, to her long, shapely legs, she was one well-built woman.

This couldn't be Meg. But Trey knew it was, without a doubt. He'd seen the hint of those long legs in her jeans while she covered the rest with a big, shapeless shirt. He'd felt those curves beneath his fingers when he'd danced with her.

So why had she been hiding it under the unbecoming clothes she wore? Bad taste? That didn't seem likely.

Knowing he should turn around and go back to the house, he couldn't move. He watched, hypnotized by the sight of the woman in the chair. Her animated face changed from smiles to frowns, as it always did. It was Meg, all right, down to the quirky smile she had when she was thinking. And yet, to him, it wasn't Meg. It couldn't be.

She tossed the phone to the sofa, then pressed her face into her hands. Her shoulders raised and lowered with a sigh, the towel straining at her breasts. With a shake of her head, she lowered her feet to the floor and stood, glancing around the room as if it were the first time she'd seen it.

When she turned to walk to the bedroom area, Trey had to swallow to breathe. That walk was unmistakably Meg, but more so now that he could actually see the seductive movement of her body. No more hints, no more suggestions. The real thing.

It occurred to him that all he had to do was take the few steps to the door and knock. Just knock on the door and Meg would come to answer it. But he shook his head. He wouldn't be able to say a word. He was having enough trouble just thinking of words that weren't associated with body parts and…sex. He knew it was a natural reaction, but there was something unnatural about it, too. At least for him. Even if she put on a robe before answering the door, he knew he wouldn't be able to put the image of her in that chair out of his mind. He might never be able to.

Forcing himself to take several steps back, he took a deep breath and closed his eyes. Oh, yeah. There she was. Burned into his mind for all eternity. And he was supposed to spend all day and all night with her tomorrow on the trail ride?

The groan that came out of him sounded like a wounded animal, even to his own ears. He breathed in and out, trying to slow his heartbeat, trying to get his body to listen to his commands. When he opened his eyes again, the lights in her cabin were out, and there were no signs of her anywhere. But he could have sworn she'd crawled inside him. She was getting to him, all right. And he'd better get a grip by morning.

With a grunt, he headed back to the house. Once inside, he went directly to the liquor bottle on the bookshelf and picked it up with fumbling fingers. After searching for a glass and finding one, he poured the golden liquid to the halfway point and lifted it to his lips.

The first swallow burned its way down his throat and went straight to his gut. But the fire of the bourbon couldn't match the fire that had already been lit and spread throughout every nerve in his body.

"Meg all right?"

Trey spun around to see Chace leaning against the door frame, and he spilled the liquor on his shirt. Ignoring it, he took two more drinks before lowering the glass. "Yeah, she's...fine," he managed to say. He flinched at his choice of words. *Fine* didn't even come close to describing Meg. She was more of a little darlin' than even his little darlin's were. And he had never—never—thought of Meg that way.

Chace looked at the glass in Trey's hand, then up at him. "You think you oughta be doing that with the trail ride tomorrow?"

Trey finished the drink, and then turned around for the bottle. "I think it's exactly what I need."

"Oh, boy," Chace said from behind him.

When Chace took the glass and bottle from his hand, Trey didn't object. Drinking himself numb wasn't the answer. Chace was right. They had a full day lined up tomorrow. Facing it with a hangover wasn't going to help the Triple B.

"Wanna talk about it?" Chace asked.

Trey shook his head.

Chace replaced the bottle on the bookshelf. "Then I'll head on up to bed. If you need anything…" He shrugged.

"Yeah. I'll be okay." Trey tried to smile, but found it impossible.

When Chace had gone, Trey collapsed onto the nearest chair and dropped his head into his hands. If he could have explained things to his brother, he would have. But the words he needed just weren't there. He'd never been so confused. He should've seen it coming. When he'd first laid eyes on Margaret Chastain, he'd known there was something not right about her. Her movements were too graceful. Too…seductive. No matter how he tried to cover them.

But one look in those grass-green eyes of hers had set the hook. Like a trout who'd taken the bait, he'd fought it, telling himself it was a passing attraction. A fluke. He'd been working too hard getting ready for this group of guests. Everything had gone wrong that morning. The pressure was on and she was the handiest candidate to help take his mind off things.

She'd reeled him in, slowly. Hook, line and sinker. Even though he'd kept telling himself she wasn't his type, he hadn't been able to stay away. Why? What was it about this woman that had him thinking about her when his mind should have been on more important things? He had started to think he had her figured out. But now, he just wasn't sure. He had questions, all right. And two whole days to get some answers.

Chapter Eight

Meg wasn't feeling at all sure of herself as she pulled her cabin door shut behind her and hurried to join the other guests at the corral. *Thankful* was the first word that popped into her head when she noticed that the sun was just beginning to peek over the horizon. In spite of the fact that she had overslept, her tardiness just might not be noticed. Which would be a good thing. The last person she wanted to have a run-in with was Trey Brannigan.

Stringing the two names together gave her a chill. How could she have been so blind?

"Your horse is ready, Miz Chastain," Pete told her as she hurried past him.

"Thanks, Pete," she said, slowing her steps. "Is Ellie in the barn?"

"Last time I saw her she was."

Meg picked up her pace and quickly scanned the

corral for signs of Trey. Breathing a sigh of relief that he was nowhere in sight, she entered the barn—and collided with a strong, broad chest.

"You're late."

There was no denying the voice. The memory of it had kept her tossing and turning all night.

Taking a breath, she looked up, while a pair of strong hands kept her from losing her balance and held her in place. Even in the early morning darkness of the barn, she could see his face clearly. His blue eyes were partly hidden by the brim of his cowboy hat, but his gaze burned into her.

"I'm sorry, I—"

"Trey, Chace needs you," one of the hands said from behind her.

Trey looked up and past her. "Yeah. I'll be there."

"He said now, boss."

The blue-eyed gaze met hers again and held it. Meg wasn't sure if it was because he was so close or if it was something in his eyes she couldn't read, but she held her breath. Waiting.

He dropped his hands. "Okay."

As he stepped around her and followed the ranch hand out into the corral, Meg stood motionless, certain her heart had stopped. Whatever it was she had seen in his eyes and the set of his jaw, she had the distinct feeling it wasn't good.

But before she had a chance to give it any more thought, Ellie appeared, leading Moonlight. "Better hustle," Ellie told her and handed her the reins. "We've been wondering what was keeping you. Are you okay?"

"I'm fine. I overslept."

Flashing her a quick smile, Ellie placed an insulated water bottle into the saddle bag. "Ranchin' starts early."

"You're coming along, aren't you?"

"Only for a little while. I want to make sure everybody remembers everything I taught them."

Meg nodded as she slipped her booted foot into the stirrup. "I'm sure we will. At least I hope so."

Ellie patted her shoulder. "You'll do fine. And I'll see you on the trail. I need to get everyone rounded up so we can get started."

Meg watched her leave before swinging up and into the saddle. "Well, Moonlight, I guess this is it," she said, more to herself than to her horse. It saddened her to think that the week was coming to a close. As she rode out of the barn to join the others, she thought about the phone conversation she had had with Geraldine the night before. She had been as honest as she possibly could, admitting that she had made friends with many of the ranch employees and that she hoped she would be able to write an unbiased article. Geraldine seemed to have more faith in her than she had in herself, and assured her that she wouldn't have given Meg the assignment if she hadn't thought Meg would do a professional job. Which only made the pressure greater.

Janet Henderson waved to her. "I was afraid you were going to miss this," she called as Meg joined the others. "I feel like a kid at Christmas, I'm so excited."

"Me, too," Meg replied. She was surprised to note that she *was* excited about the trail ride. Her plan was to add the experience to her article on the ranch. Bits and pieces of what she wanted to write kept running through her mind. She had already made several pages of notes and would put it all together when she stopped at a motel on her way back home.

A shrill whistle caused Moonlight to whinny and move beneath her. Meg patted his neck to soothe him and looked up toward the front of the group where Trey sat tall in the saddle. Quickly reminding herself to forget about the cowboy and keep her mind on business, she concentrated on what he was saying.

"Ellie will be riding with us for an hour or so," Trey announced to the group. "If you're going to have any problems, they'll happen in that first hour. Just give her a shout and she can help with anything." His sexy grin broke out. "Course you can always count on any of the rest of us, too."

Meg didn't expect any trouble beyond a good case of saddle sore by the time they returned to the ranch, but she would deal with that when she had to.

"This is the time to back out, if you're gonna do it." Trey looked directly at Meg, locking his gaze with hers, as if he was daring her to chicken out.

Meg gave him stare for stare, pulled herself up to her full mounted height and raised her chin defiantly. Whatever his problem with her was, he wasn't going to bully her into quitting. She was eagerly looking forward to this special outing.

Breaking the connection, Trey turned to the others. "If all y'all are ready, we'll get this trail ride started," he said with a shrug of his shoulders and another broad grin. Turning his horse, he led them out of the corral and into the wide open spaces.

Meg made a quick count of the number of participants, noting that only Carrie's grandmother wasn't along for the ride. Quite a turnout, she thought, but she was waiting to see if everyone wore the same look of pleasure when they returned to the ranch the next day. Only then would she be able to truthfully report whether or not the trail ride had been a success.

Janet and Ted Henderson joined Meg, and the three of them talked about the plans they had, once they all returned home.

"One thing is for sure," Ted said, "I'm going to tell all the guys in the tower about this place."

Janet's look of shock was comical. "Are you saying I was right?"

Her husband laughed. "Why, honey, you're always right."

The look between the two of them had Meg yearning for the kind of relationship they shared. As if in answer to her wishes, Trey joined them, and she once again found herself dealing with her racing heart.

"You folks doin' okay?" he asked, fully including the Hendersons, yet not quite shutting out Meg.

"Ted was just saying how relaxed he's been since we arrived," Janet answered. "You have no idea what that means to me. With his job, I worry so much about his health. For us, this trip has been a lifesaver."

"I'm glad to hear that," Trey said.

Ted nodded. "I'll be letting everyone I know in on the Triple B Ranch. Before you know it, you'll be having controllers from all over the country coming to stay."

Trey laughed. "Well, I can't say I'm not glad to hear that, either. We're all just glad to know you're enjoying yourself."

He glanced at Meg. "How about you? Enjoying yourself?"

"Tremendously," she answered. If only she knew what was causing him to act so strangely toward her. Trey had run hot and cold, and even though she knew she was a fool to care, one way or the other, it bothered her. What could she have done?

Trey answered with a brief nod and turned his attention back to the Hendersons. "We'll be stopping before too long so everyone can stretch their legs a bit. If you're hungry, there'll be biscuits and some of Theresa's famous sandplum jelly to tide you over until lunch."

Meg remained silent while the Hendersons thanked him again. Her irritation grew when he rode away with barely a nod in her direction. *Of all the—* She'd had enough. Whatever it was that had gotten him in this mood, she would... Well, she would just find out and put a stop to it, that's all.

Excusing herself from Janet and Ted, she urged Moonlight into a trot and followed Trey. With luck, he was riding alone, so their conversation—if he participated—would be private. She had promised herself that she would keep her distance where Trey was concerned, but she couldn't and wouldn't let this go on. This wasn't business. This was personal, and she would keep the two separate.

She slowed Moonlight to a walk as she approached Trey. He looked over his shoulder, but didn't stop, so she pulled alongside him, ready to do whatever it took before she lost her nerve.

Knowing it was now or never, and not wanting to leave the ranch tomorrow with bad feelings between them, she gathered her courage and turned to look at him.

"I'd like a moment with you, Mr. Brannigan."

Trey had known the moment was coming as soon as Meg had collided with him in the barn. He hadn't decided how he was going to handle his discovery of what he now thought of as "the real Meg". But it didn't look as if she was going to let him think on it any longer.

"Whatever you want, Miss Chastain." He looked her over, top to bottom, slowly and with a curiosity that he had never experienced before. Yeah, he needed to find out why this woman chose to hide herself. Maybe that would lead him to the answer of why he found her so damned attractive. Not that he believed it would, but it was damn sure worth a try.

"What I want is to know what has you running hot and cold with me," she demanded.

Was that what he'd been doing? He hadn't really thought about it like that, but maybe it was how she saw it. He just hadn't been able to stay away from her the way he had planned to. The way he needed to. It sure wasn't a very gentlemanly way to be acting toward a lady. And he didn't have an answer for her.

"One minute you're acting as if I barely exist, and the

next you're—" The hint of a blush colored her cheeks and she ducked her head.

"Kissing you?" he finished for her. They might as well get this out in the open and admit that there was definitely some strong chemistry going on. When she looked at him and nodded, he shook his head. "I don't know. But before we get into a debate about my behavior, I have a question for you."

"If you're going to ask me if I like it when I kiss you—"

"Nope that isn't it, but now that you mention it…" He couldn't contain his grin. He was more than ready to hear what she thought and felt when their lips met. Hell, he was more than ready to do some chemistry experiments right then. Just as he had figured, he hadn't been able to get the picture of her in that towel out of his mind. And the more he thought about it, the crazier it made him. He didn't like being crazy. And that made him mad as hell.

Reining in his horse, he decided there was no time like the present to get the story from her. He hoped he could trust her to tell him the truth, but he wasn't even sure of that anymore. The other riders were now farther ahead and wouldn't notice if they weren't among them. At least not until Ellie called for everyone to take a rest.

Meg came to a stop, too, waiting while he dismounted. He held on to her horse while she slid to the ground, but this time, he let her do it on her own. He didn't trust himself to touch her.

"Why are we stopping?" she asked, crossing her arms and tilting up her chin.

"Worried that you'll miss out on the biscuits?" He turned to ground tie the horses, conveniently hiding his smile. He knew body language, and she was on the defensive. Which was just fine with him. He didn't need a wildcat on his hands before he even got started.

"Maybe," she replied.

He turned back to her in time to see her fighting a smile. "Then we'll make it quick."

"Okay."

Trey stuffed his hands in his back pockets, gaining a few seconds to get his thoughts together before jumping in to what might be either a very disappointing conversation or a very interesting one. "I stopped by your cabin last night to make sure you were okay."

"Okay about what?"

"Let's just say you seemed a little shook up when I told you who I am."

Even behind her big glasses, her eyebrows noticeably drew together. "I should've realized you were Buford Brannigan," she said with a shrug. "But it wasn't like I was in a state of shock or anything."

"No? Well, I don't know why you would've been. But you did react more than I would've thought. So I wanted to be sure you were okay."

"And?"

He wasn't sure exactly what he should tell her, so he finally decided on the truth, but not directly. If she was already on the defensive, he was more than ready to be on the offensive. "Why are you hiding?"

She stiffened, and then relaxed, but her arms remained crossed in the age-old pose of protection. "H-hiding? What makes you think I'm hiding?"

Rocking back on his heels, he squinted at the bright morning sun. "I was going to knock, but…" Looking back at her, he caught her gaze and held it.

After a moment, she broke the eye contact. "You should have, if I was still up. Then you would've seen that I was fine."

"You were still up. And you were fine. Mighty fine."

She stood perfectly still, and he could almost see the wheels of her mind turning. She dropped her arms to her sides and huffed out a sigh of what he guessed was exasperation. "Get to the point, Trey."

If she was exasperated, he was chomping at the bit. But as far as he was concerned, she had deceived him. For that, she deserved a little cat and mouse. "You were on the phone. Does that ring a bell?"

"In my room? Well, yes, I do remember. I'd taken a shower and called…home. And then I went to bed. I don't have a clue what 'mighty fine' might mean…" Her voice trailed off to nothing and the silence between them grew long and heavy. Wariness and a touch of fear lit her green eyes. She was catching on. "Is there some rule against having a cell phone?" she asked.

Trey knew a dodge when he saw one. "Course not."

"Then what are you getting at?" When he didn't answer immediately, she moved and jerked Moonlight's reins free. "I hate game playing, so either get to the point or forget it."

Was it frustration or fear? Trey wasn't sure. But he knew he'd said enough to make her uncomfortable. It was time to stop beating around the bush and get the answers he so desperately needed.

"No games, then," he conceded. "Not from me. But what about you?"

She gave him a withering look and turned to grasp the pommel, ready to mount. Trey took two steps and placed his hand on hers. She froze, but she didn't turn to face him.

"Take a good look at me, Meg," he said, keeping his voice low. "I'm pretty much a 'what you see is what you get' kinda guy. No illusions. No hiding. Just me."

She relaxed beneath his touch, but just as quickly stiffened again. "And letting me believe you were nothing more than a ranch hand, or maybe even the foreman, wasn't an illusion?"

He reached out with his free hand and turned her head to face him. A hint of tears glittered in her eyes and all his anger drained away. "Aw, Meg, I never knew you didn't know who I was. But you—" He shook his head. "That towel you were wearing didn't leave much to the imagination."

Her mouth formed an *O* of surprise and her eyes widened. "I— Oh."

Taking the reins from her, he eased her away from her horse and secured the animal again. "Not that I didn't suspect something was up," he continued. "I knew the first time I helped you down from Moonlight that nothing about you was what it seemed to be."

But what he didn't tell her was that even before that, she had gotten to him. Crazy as it was, a woman so completely different from all the women before her had managed to get to him. And then to find out that she wasn't so very different after all, well, it didn't make sense to him. Not one bit.

Stopping, he turned to look at her. "All I want to know is, why?"

She lowered her head, shaking it and letting out a long, tired sigh. "It's a long story," she said, raising her head to meet his gaze. "But nobody here knew me when I arrived. For once, I wanted to be accepted for who I am, not what I look like. You're a very handsome man. Surely you can understand that."

He raised one shoulder in a half-shrug. "I never gave it much thought. I always thought it was my charm," he added, grinning. Her weak smile wasn't much compensation for his even weaker joke. He knew he and his brothers shared the Brannigan good looks. At least that's what people had told him. But there were plenty of good-looking men, from what he heard women say. He really hadn't thought about it, he'd just been himself. Always.

"I knew you wouldn't understand." Sighing, she took a step to turn away.

He reached out and touched her arm to stop her. "Wait." Pulling off his hat, he raked his fingers through his hair. This was going to take more thinking than he had planned. "I guess I can see where you're coming from. And I have to say that you sure accomplished what you set out to do. But there's still one more thing."

It was pretty clear that she wasn't comfortable with answering any more questions. But he didn't have a choice, so he waited until she finally gave a nod he almost missed.

"What about that phone call?"

"I told you. I called home."

He shook his head, hating to press her, but needing the answer to his other perplexing question. "No, the one you took in the office. Right after you learned that I'm…"

"Buford?"

Her smile was wide and genuine, and he figured he deserved the ribbing. Out of habit, he looked around to see who might be listening. How the hell had his daddy and granddaddy managed?

"The call was from a neighbor," she continued without prodding. "I live with my aunt, and she has severe asthma. The neighbor called to tell me that he'd had to take her to the hospital for an inhalation treatment."

"I'm sorry to hear that." He felt shame in asking, and for thinking it might have been something completely different. Like a boyfriend or— Hell, he was losing it. When had it ever mattered if one of his little darlin's was seeing someone else? What made Meg so different? "Is she okay?"

Meg nodded. "As okay as can be expected. It's the air quality where we live. Nothing that most people have problems with, but Aunt Dee's asthma is affected by it. Someday…"

"Someday, what?"

She gave him a sad smile. "Someday I hope we can move to a place where she can breathe without a struggle. I owe her that, and so much more."

"She must be pretty special to you."

The love in her eyes tugged at his heart, especially when her smile brightened. "She raised me from the time I was ten years old. My mother died three months before that, and my dad, well, he left when I was a baby. My stepfather tried, but he didn't have a clue how to raise a young girl."

"So he took you to live with your aunt."

"Well, actually, Aunt Dee came and got me and took me home with her. I finally found out what being happy meant. And now I'd just like to make her life easier and happier, too."

Later, as they caught up with the others and stopped for a light breakfast, Trey silently considered everything Meg had told him. He couldn't recall ever meeting anyone, man or woman, with a heart as big as hers. Knowing that didn't help his situation at all. It only made things more difficult for him. He liked Meg. Really liked her. In spite of the fact that she hadn't been who he thought she was. Or had she? He was more confused than ever. But did it matter? She would be leaving sometime tomorrow. Life at the Triple B would go on as usual and, in time, a new little darlin' would have him forgetting all about Meg. On one hand, he had discovered that she was the type of woman he was usually attracted to, but on the other, she still struck him as the marrying kind. And he wasn't. So it didn't matter. It couldn't.

Meg hated lying more than anything in the world. She should have known that this assignment would have her doing things that made her uncomfortable and went against her personal morals and standards. But if she was honest with herself, she would have to admit that she had been almost grateful for the disguise Geraldine had insisted she adopt. Her boss had reminded her that a small staff picture had appeared in the magazine several times, with reporters in disguise, but not office workers. Meg could be easily identified. In fact, Geraldine's exact words had been, "Anybody who saw it would remember that body and long, dark hair. You'll need a disguise." Bottom line was that *Trail's End* reporters were to remain unknown.

"You're awful quiet," Trey, riding beside her, said.

She turned to offer him a smile. "I think the early hour thing this morning is catching up with me."

"Maybe you can catch a few winks after lunch while we're rounding up the cattle to move on."

"I just might do that."

He looked off to his left, as if studying the terrain. "Won't be long now. Just over that ridge over there." He pointed to a spot that, to her, looked about two blocks away.

"That's great. I'm hungry."

He tugged his hat lower and chuckled. "Well, don't expect a gourmet meal. But if you like sandwiches, you're in for a treat. Now, supper will be different. But that may not be until dark. Think you can hold on until then?"

"I guess I don't have a choice," she answered, laughing. "But since I've never gone hungry once at the Triple B, I trust you."

He turned to look at her and was silent for a moment. "Good."

She had the distinct impression he wasn't talking

about the meals. That brought up things she didn't want to talk about, much less think about.

"I need to let everyone know the plan," he told her, "and then the boys and I will be dealing with the cattle. I'll catch up with you later."

Meg was almost relieved as she watched him ride away. Trust wasn't an issue she felt comfortable with at the moment. She had told Trey as much of the truth as she could. She just hadn't mentioned her job. If she passed this test, she would talk to Geraldine about the disguise. As an upstart, she doubted she could get company policy changed, but it would be worth a try. And as far as Trey was concerned, in all likelihood he would eventually learn the rest of the truth, but by then, she'd be long gone.

The thought didn't cheer her as she joined the other guests, who were busy picking out spots to enjoy their lunch. Dismounting, she tried to shake her blue mood. Luckily, Janet Henderson waved to her to join them, and Meg's good humor started to return, making it easier to offer Janet and Ted a genuine smile.

"You and Trey Brannigan seem to have hit it off," Janet said as she handed Meg a napkin.

Wanting to play down her attraction to the cowboy, Meg shrugged. "In spite of our completely different backgrounds, we have a lot in common. It's nice to make a new friend so far from home."

"Maybe you can keep in touch," Ted suggested.

Meg seriously doubted that, beyond a scathing letter from Trey, if even that, the two of them would have any communication. "Maybe," she fibbed, adding another mark to her already besmirched soul.

Ted gave her an encouraging smile, and then left to retrieve their lunch from the packhorse. Meg knew better than to hope for anything, except that maybe Trey would eventually forgive her for her deception.

"You're a very lucky woman, Janet," Meg told her. "Ted is obviously a good man."

Janet nodded. "But you're seeing him at his best, believe me. Not that he's an ogre, but his job is so stressful that he's often short-tempered. After ten years of marriage, I'm used to it."

"I guess none of us are perfect," Meg said, more to herself than to her new friend.

"No, we're sure not," Janet said with a rueful chuckle. "And before I forget, let's keep in touch after this week. Maybe we can all do this again sometime. Ted and I have talked about returning to the Triple B as soon as we can."

Ted walked up with his hands full of wrapped food. "If the size of these are any indication, and knowing Theresa probably prepared them, I'd say we're in for a treat."

Meg took the package he offered her and unwrapped it to find a huge sub sandwich. "I don't think we'll have a problem waiting for supper," she said, laughing. She was more than ready to enjoy her lunch, but she remembered she had left her water bottle in her saddlebag. "Be right back," she told the Hendersons and hurried to where she had tethered Moonlight.

She had just pulled the bottle from the bag when she looked up to see little Carrie a short distance away, struggling to control her black and white horse. The little girl looked so small on the back of the mare, Meg was concerned. She looked around to see if anyone more experienced was close enough to help, but everyone else was busy with their lunches. She took two steps in Carrie's direction, but was too late. Carrie and her horse had taken off at a fast gallop!

Too frightened to think of anything but saving the girl, Meg dropped her water bottle and scrambled to mount Moonlight. Her hands shook, but she ignored her fear and urged her horse to move. As they picked up speed, she spied Trey with the other ranch hands. All she could do was hope that he might hear her and help.

"Trey!" she shouted, praying the light wind didn't carry her words away. Her next prayer was that she would be able to stay on her now galloping horse. "Trey! Help!"

Chapter Nine

Trey heard a cry for help and looked up from the rope he was twirling to see Meg on a wild ride to...where? He started running for Temptation, gathering the dragging rope that trailed behind him into a circle. What the hell did she think she was doing? She didn't have the experience to ride at that breakneck pace. As he mounted his horse, he could see not only Meg's dust, but the dust from another rider—on a black and white pinto. His heart stopped but somehow his body kept moving.

As he began to close the distance between himself and Meg, she was closing the distance between herself and Carrie. But he knew that Meg didn't have a clue about what to do if and when she caught up with the little girl. She'd be lucky if she could slow Moonlight down. Anything could happen. And it scared him spitless.

He heard a noise behind him and saw several riders following. Not that they could do much. Ahead, he watched as the nose of Meg's horse reached even with the back of Carrie's. He caught sight of Carrie's loosened right stirrup bouncing against the horse's side. He could tell Meg was shouting to the girl. Carrie looked around and he nearly died when she began to teeter in her saddle. Everything began to move as if in slow motion. The little girl righted herself, although Trey had no idea how, given the speed at which she was riding. Meg and Moonlight slowly began to gain on the pinto. Trey was getting close enough to them to see that Carrie was trying her best to pull up on the reins and hang on for dear life at the same time. His heart lodged permanently in his throat when he saw Meg reach out for the child.

Urging Temptation even faster, he finally came within shouting distance of Meg. "Relax!" he yelled to her. "Don't reach for Carrie! Just hang on!"

For a short time during his brief stint with rodeo, he had been a pick-up man, helping bronc riders like his brother Chace off their rides. There was a huge difference between a bucking bronc and a runaway horse, and he doubted the experience would do him a lick of good in this situation. But he had to try. With luck, Temptation was the horse he could count on to stay steady and not unseat him.

Moonlight was now even with Carrie's horse, and Trey knew it wouldn't take much for him to draw up beside them. Both of the runaway horses were beginning to lose steam. They were slowing down. Not much, but at least enough that a rescue might work—*if* his timing was right, and *if* Temptation's stamina held out like he hoped it would.

"When I hold out my arm, grab on," he told Meg as he pulled even with her. "Get on behind me and hang on."

Testing Temptation, he balanced himself in the saddle, gripping his horse with his knees. The animal didn't respond to the pressure, and Trey sighed with relief. With the reins in his left hand and gripping the saddle horn with the same, he took a deep breath. *First try,* he whispered. *We have to do it on the first try.*

Leaning as much as he dared, he reached out his arm toward Meg. For a moment, she didn't move, and he feared she was too afraid to even try. He knew this took courage on her part, but it also took a positive mindset. Think about falling, and a person very well might do just that.

Meg moved, scooting to her left in the saddle and eyeing the distance to Trey. He was sure the empty space filled with dust between them probably looked something like the Grand Canyon to her, but she showed no emotion. She reached out to him with one hand while still holding the reins with the other.

"Let go, darlin'" he said, but he didn't know if he'd whispered it or shouted it. She hesitated for a split second and he shouted this time. "Come on, sweetheart. Do it now!"

He felt her hand touch his arm, then the weight of her body pulling at it. With every ounce of strength he could gather, he swung his arm and her behind him. He felt her grip his left shoulder and he nearly lost his balance, but he quickly pulled his other arm from her grasp and grabbed at the saddle horn with both hands. His vision blurred and cleared again.

Meg was safe. But he couldn't stop and congratulate himself on a job well done until he could retrieve Carrie.

Without a rider, Moonlight dropped back and Trey urged his horse closer to the pinto. The one piece of luck was that the loose stirrup was on the horse's right side, not the left where it might hit against Temptation. But with Meg hanging on to him from behind, he wasn't sure how he would grab Carrie without all of them getting tossed and probably trampled.

There was only one way they could do it.

The pinto began to slow, and Trey sent a silent thank you to his Maker. "Meg!" he shouted over his left shoulder. She leaned forward, her cheek brushing his. "Lean to your left while I lean right and grab Carrie."

When she didn't respond, he was afraid she hadn't heard him. But instead of replying, she began to do as he had instructed. With no time to think about it, he freed his right hand again, praying Meg would be able to balance them.

"I'm going to grab you, honey," he shouted to Carrie. "Don't be scared, but it might hurt a little."

Carrie, her eyes wild, stared at him. Her face was deathly pale, and her freckles stood out on the bridge of her nose like ants marching across a barren desert.

"Did you hear me?" he shouted to her.

Finally, she nodded.

"Take it easy and relax. We'll be just fine, real soon."

With the pinto now going at what Trey judged as half

the speed she had been, he felt more confident that his plan would work. "Okay, are you ready?"

Carrie nodded again, and set her mouth in a firm line of determination.

"Good girl," he said, smiling at her. "On the count of three. One." He reached out his arm, leaning to the right while Meg counterbalanced his weight.

"Two," he said simply as a get-ready measure, and took a deep breath.

"Three."

His reach wasn't quite as far as he had thought, and he had to grab the right side of Carrie's shirt instead of reaching far enough to wrap his hand around her waist as he had planned. But there wasn't any way to try again without endangering them all. In one smooth motion, he pulled her toward him. As he straightened in the saddle, Meg did, too. *Damn, she's smart.*

He settled Carrie in front of him, keeping his arm around her, and began to slow Temptation. The pinto was several yards behind them, having slowed almost to a stop without a rider.

When he was finally able to bring Temptation to a walk, he turned to see a group of riders heading toward them. Circling the horse to face the others, he stopped and waited for them to catch up.

"You just about gave us all a heart attack," Pete, the first to reach them, told him. His face was ashen beneath the stubble of his beard, and he shook his head, letting out a long relieved sigh as he dismounted. Reaching out his arms, he took Carrie from Trey. "You all right, honey?" he asked her.

To Trey's relief, she nodded. Tears sparkled in her eyes, but she sniffed them back. "Is Carrots all right?" she asked.

For a moment, no one made a sound. Then Pete began to chuckle, and the others joined in. "That pinto is just dandy," Pete answered.

Chace approached them, shaking his head. "Wish I'd had a video camera," he told Trey. "Don't believe I've ever seen anything like that. You sure got better than the last time we rodeoed together."

Weak with relief that it was all over, Trey couldn't do anything but laugh. But he wasn't immune to the feel of Meg's arms wrapped around him. When his laughter was spent, he turned his head to her. "You did real good, darlin'."

"Let me help you down, Miss Chastain," Chace offered.

Trey felt her warmth leave him and looked down in time to see her leg buckle when her feet hit the ground. Chace steadied her.

"You're hurt," Trey said, hurrying to dismount. Chace was staring at her, and then glanced at Trey. "What is it, darlin'? Your ank—"

She had turned to look at him, and he was speechless at what he saw. Her curly brown hair had slipped up and to the side, revealing smooth, dark hair beneath.

A wig?

She turned to look at Chace, obviously realizing something was wrong. Reaching up to her forehead, her fingers skimmed the smooth hair, and her face paled. Without a word, she grabbed the curls and pulled off the wig. She ducked her head, but it didn't hide the twin spots of color on the cheeks of her now white face.

"I think it's her ankle," Chace said, his voice sounding strained. "I'll take her and Carrie back to the ranch." He turned to Meg. "I hope you don't mind getting on a horse again, Miss Chastain. It's the only means of transportation we have. It'd take too long to get a truck out here."

Meg nodded. "I understand."

Pete handed Carrie to Janet Henderson. "I'll get that ice pack so's we can keep the swelling down. Get her boot off, Chace."

While the others ministered to Meg, Trey stared, unable to speak. *Why was she wearing a wig?* he wanted to shout. But he couldn't. The words might form in his mind, but his lips wouldn't follow suit.

Watching as Pete settled a subdued Meg and a still-shaken Carrie on Moonlight, with the pinto tied behind, Trey tried to sort through what had happened and what it might mean. He could only guess, and if it was what he suspected...

Chace led the mounted pair away, promising to report back on Meg's injury as soon as they knew something. The reminder that Meg was hurt didn't help Trey's mood. Neither did the group of people standing around, staring at him. His only thought at the moment was that, for the second time in his life, he had been duped by a woman and had let his body rule his brain.

He looked at the gathering that seemed to be waiting for something. "I hope to hell somebody's been keeping an eye on the cattle," he said, then turned and walked away.

* * *

Arriving back at the ranch as the afternoon began to turn to evening, Meg knew one thing. She would be eternally grateful to Chace Brannigan for never once letting on that the sight of her with her wig in her hand had been a shock. It had been written all over his face. And Trey's, too. But she didn't want to think about Trey. Not now. Maybe not ever. And she certainly didn't want to face him again.

Ellie met them at the corral with two cowboys in tow that Meg didn't recognize. "Take it easy with the ladies," she told them as they moved to help Carrie down from the horse. Her eyes widened when she looked directly at Meg, then her gaze dropped to the wig in Meg's hand. But instead of mentioning it, she turned to Chace. "Since the boys are back from the hospital and feeling fine," she said with a grin at the two, "I sent Red out to help with the cattle. And Doc Martin is on his way to check Meg and Carrie."

"I'm fine," Meg protested. "Nothing more than a twisted ankle. The ice pack has helped tremendously."

"That's a relief," Ellie said, gracing her with a smile, "but I want to make sure, so humor me, okay?"

Meg replied with her own smile.

"Why don't y'all come on in the ranch house and wait for him? And I'll bet you're hungry, too. Theresa put the leftovers from lunch in the refrigerator."

Meg's appetite had died long ago. "Nothing for me," she said.

Ellie put her arm around her. "Something cool to drink, then."

Knowing a refusal would be rude, Meg agreed.

Mrs. Winston met them on their way to the house. At first appalled, Carrie's grandmother listened to Meg's encapsulation of the afternoon's adventure and finally agreed to join them at the house. With Chace's help, and a lot of hopping that proved to be a bit on the painful side, Meg and the others made their way to the ranch house.

The doctor, who Meg thought hid his kindness behind a gruff manner, arrived minutes later. He poked and prodded before finally pronouncing both Carrie and Meg very lucky ladies. His examination and diagnosis of Meg's ankle concurred with hers. A sprain. Painful, but not serious. Ice and elevation. Meg was especially grateful when Ellie produced a pair of crutches and offered to walk with her back to her cabin.

"I had a broken leg when I was twelve," Meg explained, "and sprained the other ankle in high school. I'm very familiar with crutches. I'll be fine on my own. I promise."

Using the crutches, Meg hobbled back to her cabin. After a quick shower, she dressed and packed, trying her best not to think about anything. That, though, was impossible. She planned to leave just as soon as she could load her car, avoiding any chance of seeing Trey again. She knew she owed him an explanation. And she would send him one, in writing, just as soon as she turned in the article.

Stepping outside, with the aid of one crutch and carrying one suitcase in the other hand, she took a deep breath. She would miss the Triple B. Trey had been right. Another day, another hour, and she would probably love it as much as he did. Too bad she would never return again. But that was the price she had to pay for the chance to make her dream come true.

Slowly and carefully making her way to her car in what little was left of the fading light, she turned her thoughts to the article she would write. Her plan was to leave immediately and stop later, down the road, at a motel, where she would compose the article that would make all the difference in the world for the Triple B. At least she hoped it would. She owed Trey that, too. And it would be the truth, every single word of it. That much, she vowed.

Struggling to balance on one foot and shove her suitcase onto the backseat of her car, she noticed a pair of headlights coming up the drive. Already exhausted by her efforts with the first of her luggage, she leaned back against the open car door and watched the vehicle's progress. She wasn't surprised when it pulled into the vacant spot next to her car, but she was curious.

The dusk of evening made vision difficult, but she could make out the tall, strong body of a man exiting the Jeep. She remained motionless, but something must have caught his attention, because he turned to her after closing his door.

"Howdy, ma'am," he said, his drawl less pronounced than Trey's. Like Trey, he reached up to touch the brim of his cowboy hat.

"Hello."

He walked around the back of his vehicle and approached her, running a practiced eye over her and her situation. "Looks like you could use a little help."

He was taller than Trey by a few inches, but the resemblance was strong. Even in the poor light, she could tell that his eyes were the same, brilliant blue, though his hair was much darker and almost black.

"I can manage, but thank you," she answered, not wanting to put him to any trouble.

"No need." He reached past her to grab the handle of her suitcase, then turned his head to look at her. "Coming or going?"

"Going."

After shoving the suitcase further into the car, he backed out and straightened. "How many more?"

"One. And a tote."

"Show me the way."

There was something about him that kept her from declining his offer. His tone was friendly, but short and matter-of-fact. Even a bit commanding.

With a shrug, she picked up the crutch and adjusted it to a comfortable position under her arm. "It isn't far," she told him.

He followed her in silence to her cabin, where she pointed out the last two pieces of her luggage. "I'll just check to make sure I have everything."

When he was gone, she debated about the key to her cabin and finally decided to leave it on the small table near the loveseat. With one last look from the doorway, she sighed and stepped outside, closing the door behind her.

By the time she reached her car, her luggage was tucked neatly onto the backseat, and the gentleman stood waiting.

"What happened to your ankle?" he asked.

Before she could answer, someone else did. "Riding accident. And why the hell didn't you tell us you were coming?"

Meg turned to see Chace and Ellie walking toward them. Just what she didn't need. All she wanted was to slip away, unnoticed. And because she had no idea when Trey might return, she needed to leave as soon as possible to avoid him.

Behind her, the gentleman chuckled. "I'm that ace up the sleeve that appears at the best—and worst—times." He turned to look at Meg and touched his hat. "Devon Brannigan, happy to be of service."

Meg wasn't surprised to learn that he was the third of the brothers. She'd already made one mistake of not noticing the resemblance. She hadn't let it happen a second time. Inclining her head, she offered her hand. "Meg Chastain. And thank you, a hundred times over."

He took her hand and gave it a friendly squeeze. "It's a pleasure, Miss Chastain. I'm sorry you're leaving."

"Leaving?" Ellie cried out. "Oh, Meg, no!"

On the other side of her car, Chace leaned down to peer in her window. "Yep, her bags are all there."

Ellie hurried around the car to give Meg a hug. "You can't leave tonight. Wait until morning, please. I'm sure everyone will want to say goodbye when they get back from the trail ride in the morning."

Especially Trey, Meg wanted to add but didn't. But he would have more to say than a simple goobye. "I feel like such a—" she wanted to say "fool", but instead said, "—klutz, what with this ankle and all. And because of it, the drive may take longer. I really do need to get back on time."

"Stay, Meg," Chace chimed in.

"I have to agree with my family," Devon said.

Ellie wouldn't let it drop. "And I have something for you up at the house. Let me go fetch it."

The Brannigans' kindness didn't ease the ache in Meg's heart. She really did need to leave, but she couldn't—she wouldn't—be so heartless as to refuse their friendship. At least not until they retired to the house, when she could then get away with what she hoped would be less fuss. She would leave, and soon. Even if she had to sneak out in the dead of night.

Meg waited for Ellie's return while the brothers talked what sounded like business. She refused to eavesdrop. She had all the information she needed for the article. Her "official visit" was over.

As Ellie appeared with something in her hand, Meg heard the sound of horse's hooves approaching at a fast clip-clop. It was Trey, she knew it. And she was trapped.

"This is for you," Ellie said, handing her the gift.

Meg took it with trembling hands. If only her heart would stop pounding! She was certain Ellie could hear it. Holding up the T-shirt Ellie had given her, tears blinded her. *My Heart Belongs on the Triple B,* it read, with a drawing of Texas and a big red heart where the ranch was located.

"Oh, Ellie," Meg said, sniffing back her tears, "I'll always treasure this. Truly."

But her words were nearly drowned out by the rider and horse as they came to a dusty halt at the back of

Meg's car. Scared of what was to come, but knowing she had to face it before moving on to follow her dream of easing her aunt's life, she wiped at her tears and turned to face Trey.

Still in the saddle, Trey looked down at Meg. He'd had several hours to cool off, but he hadn't. Questions burned in his mind, and he was going to get answers. Straight answers. Just as soon as he could get her away from Ellie and Chace and whoever that man was standing behind her.

He looked closer at the man. "Dev?"

"How's it going, baby brother?"

Trey gritted his teeth. "I may be your brother, and the youngest of us, but when are you going to stop calling me that?"

Dev looked around at the others. "Who put a burr under *his* saddle?"

Chace stepped around Ellie. "Who's watchin' over the trail ride?" he asked, ignoring Dev's question.

"Pete is," Trey answered.

Yanking his hat off, Chace glared at Trey. "Pete has enough to do. Are you telling me that you've got nine people out there who don't know a bean's worth about ranching, a hundred head of cattle and Pete watching over them all?" He slammed his hat on his head, turned to his wife and leaned down to kiss her on her cheek. "I'll see you tomorrow, Little Bit."

Trey quickly dismounted to stop his brother, but Ellie beat him to it. "You don't need to go out there, Chace. By now, they'll all be settling down for the night. Nobody is going to be riding, and I sent Red out to lend a hand. If you need to, send Johnny. But they can do it without you."

"She's right, Chase," Trey agreed. "And if you all don't mind, I'd like to have a few words with Meg."

Everyone turned to look at Meg, who was clutching something to her chest. Even in the dark, he could see her wide eyes. She looked like she was ready to run. But he wasn't about to let her do it. Not yet.

"So that's the way it is," Dev said with a chuckle.

Trey shot him a warning glance, then shared it with the other two. "Do y'all know what the word *privacy* means?"

"Well, hell," Dev swore, kicking at the ground. "I'm gonna miss all the good stuff." He turned to Trey. "You be nice to this lady, baby brother."

Nice? Trey had had enough. "I don't recall asking for your help," he told Dev through gritted teeth. "And what the hell are you doing here, anyway?"

Dev let out a long sigh. "I thought y'all might want to hear the news in person."

"News?" Ellie asked.

Chace took her hand and held it. "Is it about J.R.'s lawsuit?"

"Yep."

Nobody said a word.

"So?" Trey finally said, breaking the silence. "Tell us."

Dev leaned back against his Jeep and studied them. "There's not much to it. It's pretty simple."

"Damn it, Dev, get to the point," Trey growled.

A wicked smile spread over Dev's face. "The judge dismissed it, with a warning that if J.R. caused any more trouble in this county or in the state of Texas, he'd be sorrier than a treed coon. The Triple B is and always will be ours, boys."

For a moment, they were all silent again, then Chace hugged Ellie, Ellie hugged Dev, and Trey slapped both of his brothers on their backs, while they all talked at once. Meg was the only one who didn't move, but even she wore a smile.

Trey's celebrating didn't last long. The details weren't as important to him as something else was. "Why don't you all go on into the house?" he suggested.

When no one paid any attention to him, he approached Meg. His intention was to grab her hand and drag her away from his crazy family, until he remembered her ankle. "Give me the crutches," he told her. When she handed them to him, he picked her up. Without a word, he carried her away from the others, who didn't even notice that he was leaving.

Finding a spot where he hoped there would be some privacy, he carefully set her on a rock sticking out of the ground next to a tree. Placing the crutches out of her reach, he stepped back to look at her. "You've got some explaining to do."

Meg nodded, keeping her head lowered. "Yes, I guess I do."

He hadn't expected her to answer that way. Instead of a little fire and a sassy I-don't-have-to-tell-you-anything attitude, she was meek and agreeable. That made him mad all over again.

"I want the truth, Meg. No more lies, just the straight-out truth."

"Okay."

He waited, but she offered nothing. With a heavy sigh, he hunkered down on the ground in front of her. "Look at me," he commanded. She lifted her head and met his gaze evenly, but she still didn't speak. "Why the wig, Meg?"

"It was part of the disguise."

He wasn't buying into it and couldn't keep the sarcasm out of his voice. "To hide that body of yours so people would accept you for yourself?"

"No. Not completely. But it wasn't all lies, Trey. I just didn't tell you all of it."

Her voice was quiet, but strong, without a waver or a bit of fear in it. It made Trey uneasy. Real uneasy. "So what's the rest of it?"

Her chest rose and fell with the deep breath she took. She folded her hands and placed them on whatever it was she was holding in her lap. "Richard Emery isn't the reporter from *Trail's End*. I am."

Even though he had suspected it, somewhere in the dark corners of his mind, hearing her say it made him reel. "You."

She nodded. "Yes. I was a last-minute replacement for the man who was supposed to come. I'm just one of the secretaries at the magazine, but I asked to do it. In fact, I begged. My boss grudgingly sent me."

"You." He knew he was repeating himself, but he couldn't stop. Anger built inside him. She had deceived him from the moment she'd set foot on the Triple B. Him, and his family. Being made a fool of had never sat well with him. This time, it made him see red.

"So everything was a lie." He got to his feet, clenching his hands at his sides so he wouldn't snatch her up and hurt her the way he was hurting. "You were just trying to get a story. Right? And in the process, you made fools of us all."

"None of you are fools, Trey. You're all wonderful." She moved slowly, but finally stood, leaning against the tree for support.

He was tempted to help her. It wasn't his nature to watch a lady struggle. But he quickly reminded himself that this wasn't a lady, and he forced himself to take a step back, away from her.

Tipping her head back, she rested it against the tree trunk and closed her eyes. "If you know anything at all about *Trail's End*, you know that the identity of the reporter is never revealed until the review appears in the magazine." She opened her eyes and looked at him. "You're aware of that, aren't you?"

His nod was brief and curt. Of course he knew. But that didn't change things. Not the way he felt. "What are you going to say in the article?"

"I can't tell you that."

"You can't tell me? Or you won't?"

"I can't."

"What about the rating? What are you giving us?

She leaned forward, her features intense and unyielding. "Trey, I can't tell you that. I can't tell you anything."

"Why the hell not?" he shouted. "What difference is it going to make? We'll find out anyway, when the review comes out. Why not now?"

"Because doing so could very well jeopardize my

job. I *need* this job. Desperately." She shook her head and sighed, leaning back against the tree again. "You don't understand."

"Oh, I understand," he said. "But I can't believe you'd let that make a difference."

She stared at him. "Why?" she cried. "Why *wouldn't* it make a difference? You have your ranch. This wonderful, beautiful ranch. You have a family that cares about you and loves you. All I have is my job and my Aunt Dee. That's it. And if I lose one, I could lose the other. I can't let that happen."

Moving closer, he touched her cheek with his hand. "What about us?" he dared to whisper. "What about what's happened between us? That has to make a difference."

She didn't answer and he stood motionless, unable to breathe. He wasn't even sure why he'd said that. It hadn't come from his head. It had come from his— His heart seemed to stop as he waited.

Closing her eyes for a moment, she opened them again and met his gaze. But instead of the soft, loving look he was used to seeing in her green eyes, there was a hard glint in them. His heart kicked in, thudding in his chest.

"Nothing has happened," she replied.

Chapter Ten

"So what do you think, baby brother?"

Trey looked up from the toe of his boot, his mind on Meg. "About what?"

Chace, sitting in the chair their daddy had always favored, chuckled. "About whether or not we made a good impression on Richard Emery. After all, you were the one who was so all-fired intent on doing the Triple B proud for that five-star rating. Think we'll get it?"

Trey winced at the pain in his chest. It wasn't a real pain, it was— He shook his head. "I guess we'll have to wait and see."

Standing, he crossed the living room and placed the glass of bourbon he hadn't even bothered to taste on the wide stone mantle, and then he looked at his family. It was great to see Dev again, and the news about J.R. had been more than any of them had hoped for. But he wasn't in the mood to celebrate the victory.

"Where are you going?" Ellie asked when he turned for the door.

"Out. I need some air." He didn't bother to look at them again. They could think anything they wanted to think. He had his own thinking to do.

As soon as he stepped out onto the porch, he looked toward Meg's cabin. The lights were out, and he wondered how she was able to sleep. He had a feeling he wouldn't be getting much shut-eye before morning.

How could he have been so wrong about her?

How could such a soft, warm-hearted woman suddenly turn so hard and cold? She felt nothing for him. Nothing. Damn, he hurt. Bad. Even years ago, when he'd been the fool of the county, he hadn't hurt this bad.

But maybe if he talked to her, told her that it didn't matter if she didn't tell him about the review, maybe then he could stop hurting. And maybe then she'd be the Meg he had come to know. She wouldn't feel real kindly toward him for waking her up, but if it straightened things out, everything would be back to normal. He had just gone about asking her about the rating the wrong way. That was all. Once he made things right again, he could get back to trying to figure out why he didn't want to tell her goodbye tomorrow.

As he walked across the grass between the ranch house and her cabin, he tried out several variations of an apology. None sounded good, but he was ready to try anything. At her door, he hesitated. If he knocked and she asked who it was, he was sure she wouldn't let him in. So instead, he reached for the knob, hoping she wouldn't make a ruckus when he woke her up.

The door was unlocked. He opened it and waited for his eyes to adjust to the darker interior of the cabin, listening for any sounds from her. Being careful that he didn't bump into anything, he felt his way through the sitting area to the bedroom.

The moon was still full enough to shine in the window nearest the bed. But Meg wasn't in the bed.

He looked around, checking for signs of her, but the bed was made and the room was bare of any personal belongings, except the slight scent of Meg. But even that wasn't strong enough to indicate that she was there.

Making his way back to the sitting area, he groped for the lamp and turned it on, bathing the room in a soft glow.

The cabin looked unused, as if she had never been there.

After switching off the light, he hurried to the door and half ran to the parking area. Even before he reached it, he could see that her rust-eaten car was missing. She was gone. No goodbye, and no chance for him to try to make things right.

Anger flared inside him, blinding him. He veered to the left and nearly ran into a tree. Stopping, he realized it was the one where they had talked earlier. He slammed his fist into the trunk, letting the pain wash through him to mix with the other hurt. When it let up, he caught a glimpse of something on the ground. Bending over, he picked up the item he remembered that she had been carrying. The soft, gentle scent of her filled his head. He almost threw the bundle of cloth down again, but instead, he tucked it under his arm and headed for the barn.

He wasn't sure how long he had been sitting on the pile of sacked oats, trying to make sense of things, when Chace came looking for him.

"Hey, Trey, it's gettin' late. You ready to call it a night?"

Trey didn't even bother to look up.

"Did you find him?" Dev called from the barn door.

"Yeah, he's here," Chace answered and waited for Dev to join them. "Dev had an idea we wanted to run by you."

Staring at his hands, clasped between his knees, Trey didn't comment.

"I was thinkin'," Dev said, "if we built a hall—you know, a place where people could gather of an afternoon when it's hot outside—where they could play pool or Ping-Pong or cards or whatever. Maybe just talk, I don't know. But it would be something to add to the place."

Trey looked up at him. "You plannin' to stay?" When Dev didn't answer, Trey shook his head. "Then what the hell difference does it make to you?"

"Trey—"

"No, Chace. Dev isn't going to stay to see this through, just like always." Trey could feel Dev looking at him, and he glanced up.

"What's eatin' at you, baby brother?"

Trey looked back at his hands and the deep gashes on the knuckles of his right one. "Nothin'."

In front of him, Chace cleared his throat. "It's Meg."

"Meg?" Dev asked. "You mean that nice lady that I helped with her suitcases?"

Trey's head snapped up to stare at him. His brother had helped her leave? It figured.

"Meg was the reporter, wasn't she, Trey?" Chace asked, his voice low.

"You knew?"

Chace shrugged one shoulder. "Ellie and I were talking about it and kinda suspected she was, especially after she came back with that wig in her hands."

"Wig?" Dev asked. "Wait a second. That long dark hair wasn't any wig, I can swear to that."

"Oh, yeah?" Trey said, jumping to his feet. "And how would you know?"

Holding his hands up to stop Trey, Dev backed up a step. "Hey, hold it. Calm down, baby brother. I wasn't trying to horn in on your woman. But I do have two eyes and twenty-twenty vision."

Sinking back to the feed bags, Trey avoided looking at them. "She isn't my woman. So if you want her, you'll have to find her. She's gone."

"Damn, I was afraid of that," Chace said. "Ellie tried to talk her into staying, but that's when you showed up. What did you do to scare her off?"

"I didn't do anything," Trey said through gritted teeth. "So if Dev wants her—"

"Not me," Dev interrupted. "I do just fine without a woman. But it sounds to me like you're the one who should be going after her."

"I've already told him that," Chace said. "But do you think he'll listen to me?"

"Why should he start now?" Dev replied. "He's never listened to either one of us before this."

"Don't be a fool, Trey," Chace warned him. "I almost was."

"He is," Dev snorted. "Baby brother, you're one dumb cowboy if you don't go after that lady." He leaned forward. "What's that?" he asked, pointing at the bundle of cloth next to Trey.

"Something Meg left behind." Picking it up, Trey handed it to Chace. "Ellie can mail it to her, if she needs it."

Dev took it from Chace and held it up. "It's a T-shirt." He looked at the front of it and then turned it to show Trey. "Wonder why she left it."

"Maybe because it isn't important to her," Trey growled, snatching it out of Dev's hands. He hadn't missed the big red heart and the bold lettering. "She doesn't care about the Triple B."

And she doesn't care about me.

"Go after her, Trey," Chace said. Beside him, Dev nodded in agreement.

"I'll pass, thanks." Trey stood and tossed the shirt onto the feed bags. "I've got the Triple B, and that's all I need. Besides, there are plenty of little darlin's out there to keep me busy."

Meg juggled the packages in her arms and wrestled with her keyring, trying to find the house key. If she hadn't discovered that her last pair of pantyhose was almost in shreds, she would be packed and ready to leave for Wyoming.

Turning her wrist, she glanced at her watch. But instead of noting how late she was running, she noticed something else. *Fifteen minutes.* It had been a whole fifteen minutes since she had given any thought to Trey. She was getting better. After two weeks of trying to forget about the cowboy, she was finally able to go a whole fifteen minutes without him jumping into her thoughts. Maybe by the time she reached retirement she would pretty much have forgotten him.

Not exactly a cheery idea, she thought as she finally found the key and fit it into the lock. At least she had been able to keep the entire Triple B incident from Aunt Dee. And that hadn't been easy, when all she had felt like doing after turning in the review and article was sleep and cry. Her excuse to her aunt had been a hormonal imbalance, which hadn't been that far from the truth. The Triple B had earned its five-star rating, but the assignment had cost Meg her heart.

Turning the doorknob, she pushed open the front door and stepped into the cozy living room. "Well, I think I got everything I—"

"Hello, Meggie, dear," Dee greeted in her usual breathless way. "We have a visitor."

Meg's voice had completely deserted her. Staring at the back of the man sitting across from her aunt, she watched, speechless, as he rose to his feet and turned toward her.

"Howdy, Meg," he said, facing her and offering his sexy grin.

She glanced at her aunt and then back at him. Her heart raced. Pounded. And time seemed to stand still. "Trey," she finally managed. "What—what are you doing here?"

"Mr. Brannigan has been telling me all about his lovely ranch," Dee explained. "You never did say much about it, but it sounds as delightful as he his."

Trey turned to her. "I thought we agreed that you'd call me Trey, ma'am," he said, a teasing note in his voice.

"That's right." Dee's tinkling laughter became a gasp for air, but she quickly recovered. "As long as you remember to call me Dee."

Meg stared at the two of them. What had gone on during her short absence? She hadn't been away from the house long enough for them to become bosom buddies in— Oh, right, there was Trey's charm to take into consideration, and the fact that her Aunt Dee found a friend in everyone. *Not* what Meg needed right now.

Dee waved a hand at Meg. "Put your packages down, Meg, and go sit over there on the sofa by Trey."

Meg had to bite her cheek to keep from moaning. "I only have a few minutes," she reminded her aunt. "I have that plane to catch to Cheyenne, and I'm already running late." She hoped Trey got the message. Whatever the reason for his visit, she had things to do and places to go.

"And Trey came all the way to see you, Meg. Goodness, it certainly wasn't to see me." Dee flashed her beautiful smile at Trey.

Trey returned the smile. "But meeting you, Dee, has been a pleasure I hadn't counted on."

Dee laughed again. "And I'll bet you even charm the rattlesnakes down there in Texas."

Knowing she had to put an end to this mutual admiration society that Trey and her aunt seemed to be forming, Meg dropped her purchases at her feet and perched on the arm of the sofa. "So how are Chace and Ellie?" she asked, and avoided looking at him directly. Her heart just couldn't take that.

"Good. They're good. Ellie sure misses you though."

Dee leaned forward. "He was just telling me about how much you helped out in the office while you were there. But I told him you weren't a secretary at the magazine anymore. You've been promoted to staff reporter. And all because of his ranch."

"Congratulations, Meg," Trey said.

The tone of his voice made her look at him, and his gaze caught and held hers. She saw a mix of emotions in his blue eyes, and even thought there was a sparkle of pride there among them.

She managed to say, "Thank you," but couldn't say more. Seeing him here, in her home, was more than she could deal with. And she wished she didn't have to. Hadn't she just been congratulating herself for not thinking about him every minute of the day? How long would it take her this time to reach the fifteen-minute mark? Another two weeks? She didn't think even that would be long enough.

Glancing at her watch, she gasped. "I'll never make it!" she cried and jumped up from the sofa. Scrambling to retrieve her packages, she looked up to glare at Trey, then turned to her aunt. "I have to finish packing and then it's almost an hour drive to Midway. I'll miss my flight, I know it." Picking up the last package, she stood frozen. "What am I going to do?"

"Why don't you—" her aunt began.

"Wait! I know, I'll call Geraldine and see if we can get the flight changed." Meg dropped the packages again and hurried to pick up the phone on the end table. Dialing quickly, she waited for someone to answer. "I suppose I'll have to pay for a new ticket, but— Geraldine Martin, please. This is Meg Chastain."

It seemed like hours before Geraldine answered. "Problems, Meg?"

Meg turned her back to the room and took a deep breath. "I'm so sorry, Geraldine, but I have a surprise out-of-town visitor, and there's no way I'm going to make my plane on time."

"I see," Meg's boss replied. "That does cause us a bit of trouble, doesn't it? Or does it?"

Meg wasn't sure what she was getting at. Of course it caused trouble. It could also cause her to lose her job. "What do you mean?"

Geraldine's throaty laughter echoed over the wire. "Well, if that surprise visitor is the same sexy cowboy who stopped by here looking for you earlier, I can certainly understand why you're about to miss your plane."

Glancing over her shoulder at Trey, Meg swallowed. "He came by the office?" she asked, turning back and cupping the mouthpiece so she wouldn't be overheard.

"Not long after you left, as a matter of fact," Geraldine answered. "And I swear he would've camped out here until you returned from Wyoming if we hadn't given him your address. But don't you worry about the assignment. Karen should be checking in at the airport right about now."

"Karen? But—"

"I'm sure you and your cowboy have a lot to catch up on," Geraldine continued. "And you and I can chat about your next assignment in a few days."

Before Meg could protest, her boss had hung up. She replaced the receiver and spun around, her fury taking a strong hold on her. "You!" she shouted at Trey. "Do you have any idea what you've done?"

"Meg, I—"

"No, I don't want to hear it," she said, covering her ears with her hands. "Do you know how long it's taken me to get a position as a staff reporter?"

"A long time?"

Just as she started to tell him exactly how many years she had begged for a chance, she caught sight of her aunt, opening the door. "Where are *you* going?" she demanded.

Dee's eyes widened. "Why, I'm going to play bridge with John and Sadie and Aaron. I told you that, remember?"

"But you can't!"

Dee's left eyebrow raised. "Oh, really?"

Meg knew that look and that tone. And she knew that no amount of begging or pleading would do any good.

"Enjoy your bridge game, Dee," Trey said from behind Meg.

Unable to reply, Meg watched her aunt step through the doorway and close the door, leaving her alone to deal with Trey. Could life get any worse?

When Dee had gone, Trey touched Meg's arm, not wanting to get her any more riled up than she already was, but unable to keep from touching her any longer. "Meg."

She pulled away and faced him, fury and disbelief in

her eyes. "I can't believe this. I may lose my job over this. My job!"

He stuffed his hands in his pockets to keep from reaching out for her again and silently prayed that he could get her to listen to him. This was his last chance. His only chance. "Come back to the Triple B with me, Meg."

"And be your secretary?" Her laughter was mocking. "Not on your life. I spent eleven years as an office girl, and I've finally reached my dream." She shook her head, and her eyes glittered with unshed tears. "And now I may have lost it."

It pained him to see how much she was hurting. After meeting her aunt, he could understand her devotion to the woman who had raised her and loved her. He didn't want to do anything that would separate them. He had never planned to.

"I'm not offering you a job at the ranch," he said, keeping his voice low. Slowly, he reached up and touched her face. Her eyes softened. Not much, but enough that he knew he would get his chance.

But before he could say more, she moved away. "I can't tell you about the article, Trey. Not two weeks ago. Not today."

"I don't care about the article."

Circling around the chair, she stopped behind it, as if trying to protect herself: "But you care about the ranch."

"Of course I do." He took a step closer, wondering what he could say to get her to understand. "But I was wrong to try to force you to tell me about the review. I'm sorry for that, Meg. I truly am."

She studied him for a moment, and then lowered her head in a brief nod of acceptance. "I wish I could tell you."

He shook his head and moved closer, stopping at the edge of the chair. "It doesn't matter. Sure, a good rating could make a difference, but we'll manage okay, whatever the rating is. Besides, not everybody reads *Trail's End*," he added with a grin.

"I suppose that's true," she said, smiling back at him. "But if you aren't here to offer me a job or try to find out about the review…"

Before he could think about it and chicken out, he closed the distance between them and stood next to her. "I've come to tell you that I've missed you."

"Oh."

Was that indifference in her voice? If it was, he wasn't sure he could continue. But he didn't have a choice. Taking a deep breath, he went on. "After listening to my brothers tell me what a fool I was for letting you get away, and putting up with Ellie hardly speaking to me, well, I had to finally admit something."

"What?" Her voice was a whisper.

"It isn't a job I came here to offer you. And I know you told me that there wasn't anything between us, but you're wrong," he continued, touching a strand of her long, dark hair. "I know it. You know it. So can we forget that night ever happened?"

Pressing her lips together, she nodded. "I'd like nothing more than to do that."

"Good," he said on a sigh of relief. "I need you with me, Meg."

"But my job… Aunt Dee—"

He pressed a finger to her lips. "I have it all figured out, darlin'. What better place for Dee than the Triple B? She'll be more than welcome, and just think of how much better she's going to be. The ranch is the perfect environment for a person with her health problems. I checked into it."

She wrapped her hand around his wrist and pulled his hand away. "And I'm supposed to do what? Answer the phone and book reservations?"

She tried to move away, but he stopped her, tipping her face up to his with his thumb. Her green eyes glistened, and her lower lip trembled. He was going about this all wrong. Again. Why couldn't he get it right?

He shook his head. "No. Like I said, I'm not offering you a job. I'm offering you my love, Meg." He watched as her eyes grew wider. "Nobody will ever take your place in my heart. Believe me, I've tried." He dropped his hand and shook his head, chuckling. "Not tried to replace you," he hurried on, when he saw the look on her face. "I've just tried to stop hurtin' because you were gone. But I couldn't."

"I've been hurting, too," she admitted.

Her words touched his heart, and he felt that maybe they understood each other. Taking her hand, he led her to the sofa, where he pulled a bundle from under his Stetson. "You left this behind," he said, handing it to her.

"My shirt," she said. Holding it in front of her, she sank to the sofa. "You don't know how many times I've thought about this." A tear slid down her cheek, and she looked up at him. "How many times I've thought about you and wished I hadn't said the things I said. But I had to."

He eased down beside her and kissed a tear that glistened near her mouth. "We never said any of that, remember?" he whispered against her lips. Moving back, he took her hands in his. "Will you marry me, Meg? Will you come back to the Triple B with me and be my wife?" Before she could answer, he hurried on. "With all the computers and technology, maybe we can convince your boss that you can do your job from the ranch. What's that called?"

"Telecommuting," she said, smiling through a steady stream of tears. "And even if I couldn't—"

"I want you to have your dreams, Meg." With his finger, he traced one small, determined tear. "I'll spend the rest of my life making your dreams come true. If you'll say yes."

"Oh, Trey," she said. "Of course I'll marry you. How could I not? I do love you."

Joy coursed through him, filling him with the lightest and best feeling he had ever known. Claiming her lips, he kissed her long and hard, wishing he would never have to stop. But eventually he moved back, giving them both a moment to breathe.

Meg pulled at the shirt, wedged between them, and smoothed it out on her lap. "This says it all," she said, sighing. "My heart really does belong on the Triple B."

* * * * *

HARLEQUIN *Super*ROMANCE®

A six-book series from Harlequin Superromance.

WOMEN *in Blue*

Six female cops battling crime and corruption on the streets of Houston. Together they can fight the blue wall of silence. But divided, will they fall?

Coming in December 2004,
The Witness by Linda Style
(Harlequin Superromance #1243)

She had vowed never to return to Houston's crime-riddled east end. But Detective Crista Santiago's promotion to the Chicano Squad put her right back in the violence of the barrio. Overcoming demons from her past, and with somebody in the department who wants her gone, she must race the clock to find out who shot Alex Del Rio's daughter.

Coming in January 2005,
Her Little Secret by Anna Adams
(Harlequin Superromance #1248)

Abby Carlton was willing to give up her career for Thomas Riley, but then she realized she'd always come second to his duty to his country. She went home and rejoined the police force, aware that her pursuit of love had left a black mark on her file. Now Thomas is back, needing help only she can give.

Also in the series:
The Partner by Kay David (#1230, October 2004)
The Children's Cop by Sherry Lewis (#1237, November 2004)
And watch for:
She Walks the Line by Roz Denny Fox (#1254, February 2005)
A Mother's Vow by K.N. Casper (#1260, March 2005)

HARLEQUIN®
Live the emotion™

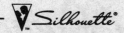

SPECIAL EDITION™

A sweeping new family saga

THE PARKS EMPIRE

Dark secrets. Old lies. New loves.

Twenty-five years ago, Walter Parks got away with
murder...or so he thought. But now his children have
discovered the truth, and they will do anything to clear the
family name—even if it means falling for the enemy!

Don't miss these books from six favorite authors:

ROMANCING THE ENEMY
by Laurie Paige
(Silhouette Special Edition #1621, on sale July 2004)

DIAMONDS AND DECEPTIONS
by Marie Ferrarella
(Silhouette Special Edition #1627, on sale August 2004)

THE RICH MAN'S SON by Judy Duarte
(Silhouette Special Edition #1634, on sale September 2004)

THE PRINCE'S BRIDE by Lois Faye Dyer
(Silhouette Special Edition #1640, on sale October 2004)

THE MARRIAGE ACT by Elissa Ambrose
(Silhouette Special Edition #1646, on sale November 2004)

THE HOMECOMING by Gina Wilkins
(Silhouette Special Edition #1652, on sale December 2004)

Available at your favorite retail outlet.

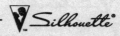